BLACK UMBRELLA STORIES

Nicolette de Csipkay

BLACK UMBRELLA STORIES

Nicolette de Csipkay

with illustrations by Francesca de Csipkay

2003

Starcherone Books
P.O. Box 303
Buffalo, NY 14201-0303
www.starcherone.com

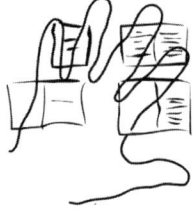

This is a work of fiction. No statement herein should be accepted as a simple statement of fact.

The author expresses gratitude to the following publications in which these pieces first appeared: *Chick Lit: Postfeminist Fiction, Gulf Coast, 90, Rohwedder, Short Story, Southern Plains Review,* and *Telescope.*

Francesca de Csipkay's illustrations accompanying the stories "The Cat Lady," "A Visit to Portugal," "Evelyn & Bill," "Wanda & her Imagination," and "How Glora Grows Long Nails" were scanned from original prints of copper-plate etchings using aquatint and hardground techniques. The reproductions are used here with permission.

Editor: Ted Pelton
Proofreader: Florine Melnyk
Cover design: Betsy Frazer

Library of Congress Cataloging-in-Publication Data

De Csipkay, Nicolette, 1960-
    Black umbrella stories / Nicolette de Csipkay ; with illustrations by Francesca de Csipkay.-- 1st ed.
        p. cm.
    ISBN 0-9703165-7-7 (alk. paper)
    1. Women--California, Southern--Fiction. 2. California, Southern--Fiction. 3. Fairy tales--Adaptations. 4. Feminist fiction, American. I. De Csipkay, Francesca, 1949- II. Title.
PS3604.E23B58 2003
813'.6--dc21

                                                2003002370

CONTENTS

for my parents, Charles and Genevra,
and for Ted

THE CAT LADY

Bored with teachers who flittered false eyelashes, sick of girls who answered their questions, and tired of girls who liked boys and boys who liked girls, Janet was passing by rows of glossy-leaved orange trees on her way home from a tenth-grade school day when she saw a small man with dark hair, a moustache and very muscular arms digging a pit in the backyard of the house with the weathervane. He was listening to a soft pop radio station, but as Janet walked by he looked up and gestured to her.

"Need some extra cash?" he asked.

"No," Janet mumbled uncertainly. "I have to go do my homework," she added in a garbled manner, so that the man did not understand her and interpreted her answer to be affirmative. Janet was a shy girl, but she had also learned that mumbling allowed her a certain freedom—the freedom to do what she wanted regardless of what she said. Janet changed words at will, misunderstanding or being misunderstood as it suited her.

"I have a sister," the man went on, "a sister who likes girls like you. Do you know any boys? She also likes boys."

Janet shook her head, but the man was already opening the gate into the backyard. From next to the shovel blared a static-ridden Tom Jones song, and the man stooped to turn down the volume. "Come in," he said heartily. "Kids like you can always use a little extra cash. And it won't be much work, no," he shook his head, laughing, "not work like I have here," he jerked his head in

9

the direction of the pit. Janet could not help her curiousity, so she followed the man into the house.

The house smelled sweet, like overripe bananas or maybe apples, but slightly nauseating to Janet because just beneath the smell there were lots of kittens milling about and two overflowing litterboxes. "My sister's in the back room," the man said, jerking his head at the wall, "but you can have something to eat first. You must be hungry after school." He took Janet's school books from her and put them on the kitchen table. "Do you like cheddar?" Janet nodded; she liked cheese. "Good," said the man, opening the refrigerator, "we've had this since last Christmas, and my sister won't eat it because she's allergic to lactic acid, and I like my hamburgers plain." The man took out a big oblong cardboard box and opened it up. "This is government cheese," the man said. "We have food stamps, too." Inside the box the cheese was covered with green mold. Matter-of-factly he took the cheese in his hand, scraped it with a knife, and then carved off a large piece for Janet. But Janet only pretended to eat it because she didn't like blue unless it was supposed to be there and once it was there you couldn't take it away. "Just a minute," said the man, "I'll go talk to my sister." When he left Janet threw the piece of cheese into an earthenware jar on top of the television in the livingroom.

She stroked one of the kittens. It had grey and white patches and blue eyes; it was very young and tried to suck at her fingers.

"Okie-dokie," she heard the man say, and then he came into the livingroom. "Go down the hall, last door to the right. My sister will tell you what she wants."

Janet put down the kitten carefully and it ran under the sofa.

The man's sister was a big fat lady lying in bed. She was naked and she had another kitten draped across her breast, pure black and purring like a pinwheel. Janet stopped at the doorway and stared at her until the lady looked up. "My you're a quiet one," she said. "Come on in and sit down, sweetie," she said, patting the bed by her side. "Do you like kittens," she said, "do you want to pet my kitty?" Janet nodded because she didn't know what to say. She petted the lady's kitten until it started to meow and began pulling itself towards her, its claws digging for a hold in the woman's soft flesh. "Naughty, naughty," the woman said, gently detaching his claws and putting him next to her on the bed, "you know better than to do that to Mama." The lady's sheets were mostly blue, with little white flowers on them.

The lady took Janet's hand and held it. "Do you have a boyfriend, sweetie?" she said. "M-mm," Janet answered. The lady put her hand on her stomach. "I have a fat tummy, don't I?" She wore a blue satin ribbon around her neck. "Do you know why? Feel my stomach," the lady said. "There — can you feel it kicking? Feel it again. Can you feel it in there?" she asked insistently. Janet looked steadily at the lady's forehead; she felt nothing, except that the lady's skin was soft, covered with a powdery, silky down. The lady prompted her hand further along. "Can you feel it here?" Janet shook her head. "Here?" "No, here," she corrected herself, "just keep your hand here and I know you'll feel it."

The lady pressed Janet's hand close to her body and Janet didn't dare move it. She saw the lady's eyelashes flutter almost shut and her mouth open slightly, her lips dark red and glistening. In the next room there were a few coughs, a toilet flush, a faucet's squeak on and off. Janet felt something move beneath her hand.

The lady made a choking noise. "Did you feel it?" she gasped, "did you feel it?" Janet nodded. "Another little one just dying to get out!" the lady said with delight. "And aren't you just a good kid! I just bet a good kid like you would go out there and bring me one of my babies back. You know the cutie with the blue eyes? It's about his dinnertime. Then you can go home if you want, sweetie, just tell my brother and he'll give you the cash."

Janet searched high and low, but she couldn't find the kitten and finally had to ask the man. "Give her this," he directed, and she took the small tiger-striped one he handed her into the lady. "Thanks, sweetie," she said, putting the kitten's mouth to her nipple, "you be sure to come back and visit us again."

Janet left the room and asked the man for money. He reached in the earthenware bowl where she had thrown the cheese. "You don't like our cheese? It's not good enough for you?" he growled, spitting on the ground and throwing her an angry glance. He pulled out a handful of quarters from the jar and held them out to her. "Now get out of here. Just get out," he repeated more quietly, looking away. Janet took the money and picked up her books.

On her way to the gate she saw a huddle of kittens at the bottom of the pit the man had been digging, the grey and white kitten curled up into a little ball on top, fast asleep. The rooster on the roof spun with a sudden whir, and Janet lifted the ponytail off of her neck. She clicked her tongue and called out "kitty," but it didn't move.

"It's no use, kid," the man said, coming from behind her and picking up the spade. "She just has too damn many of them. I just can't afford it anymore."

When Janet got home her mother was anxious. "You're late.

Your father will be home any minute and you know how angry he would have been if you weren't here."

"Well, I am here. I just went to Howard Johnson's with Evie for awhile, that's all," Janet mumbled.

"What's that? Well, you better be careful young lady, I'm warning you," her mother put her hands on her hips. "By the way, the Lenders called wondering if you could babysit tonight."

"Okay," Janet said, going into her room and shutting the door. She emptied the change out of her purse and clinked it into the fat belly of her piggy bank.

Between five and six on weekday evenings, if the sun had not set, you could look down from Janet's window on a lush green expanse of orange groves and on the sparkling, double strand of cars travelling perpetually elsewhere. Beyond that you could see the mountains rising sharply into the sky, and somewhere above that all the extra money Janet would earn and the day she would have a car like everyone else.

But a beautiful blue car with an eight-track tape-deck and windows you could open and shut by button.

THE MAGIC THIMBLE

After that they make you swallow a stone and then they push you into the pond. It is inevitable.

She views Adele Rosselini with suspicion. She sits in a green canvas director's chair outside her front door, drinking tea from a delicate rosebud porcelain cup, tapping the gilt-edged saucer which it rests upon with her thimble, and suspects.

Adele has murdered someone.

Adele suspects that Old Granny suspects her. But she suspects that she is suspected of lying. She lies on her bed, to one or two people at the same time and, at the same time, she lies with the one or two people she lies to until the phone rings and predicates her deceptions. It is always the timely ding-dong of the phone or the tower bell which reminds her of being a passive liar. The worst kind. She feels herself pushed into the pink velour bedspread as if she herself were the complementary red pillows, suitably arranged to cushion a protracted body. But beneath it all she feels her own inflexibility, her bones feel hard, they resist. Only the passive liar can feel, can know, can experience the fact that she lies, and passively.

Adele is thin, cutting the observer with her edges and forcing the eye into angles. It is this characteristic of Adele's which exposes her to Old Granny's observant eyes every time Adele walks by her director's chair. Adele looks at Old Granny's sewing basket and ripping it apart, with startling fury, she sticks all the needles into soft, plump Old Granny. This action does not hurt Old Granny, however; such things are done passively, with round phrases and circuitous questions, and even then only inside the head. (When Adele kills she remembers having killed and having been killed, having to kill and having to be killed. A deluge of killings descends upon her like a woodsman's axe, chop-chop. When Adele kills she remembers that she lives near a forest; she remembers that she is a child, drawing a line, in violent pink chalk, over cracks on a sidewalk. She walks carefully along the line, balancing each step, singing step on a crack, break your mother's back. The other little girls chime in, pigtails swinging, cherry Koolaid lips baring milky teeth, cherry tongues and throats.)

Adele lives a wonderful life. Her friends send her birthday cards and the jokes on them are not about her age. Adele does not avoid looking into the mirror, either, although she has only one mirror because she is superstitious about breaking them, and the more mirrors one has, the more likely it is that one will be broken.

The villagers had always liked her.

Once a month Adele looks into her closet and decides what she wants to throw away. One month it is three sets of pink leotards, one striped silk blouse and two pairs of trousers — one a grey wool, the other a burgundy corduroy. One month it is underwear, because she is tired of bras and panties and, even, socks. She folds them carefully into white plastic supermarket bags and deposits them into the trash receptacle at the back of the duplex. She suspects, Adele knows, and, as she passes by, Adele almost says to Old Granny, "don't worry: I have wrapped them in plastic and they are clean. I mended the holes in the purple socks, and the broken strap on the bra." Even so, as she throws the bag into the bin, Adele feels all the eyes in the woods blinking at her like Christmas lights. (Adele's mother always sews Adele's clothes. She is an expert seamstress. Adele is embarrassed because all the other little girls buy their clothes, and Adele's wardrobe, by comparison, lacks sophistication. Her mother's favorite color is red, and the bus driver can spot Adele a mile away, waving like a flag on a windy day, while immediately below her knees, only a second's peek down from her white bobby socks, for better or worse, Adele's reflection is caught forever in matching red patent leather shoes.)

The telephone (or the tower bell) rings at least thirty times a day because Adele has a wonderful life, and so much has to be predicated. Adele doesn't need to answer, of course, it is only the ringing which signifies. The managers who walk her home from their shops and offer her jobs, though Adele already has a good one, have the same significance. The newspaper which arrives at her door every morning, though she does not read it, has the same significance. Except for Old Granny, everyone believes in Adele, and belief is all that matters. But tremors travel from Old Granny's hair net down to her orthopedic shoes like a row of dominoes whenever Adele crosses her path. Granny turns as purple in the green director's chair as the pair of socks Adele discarded yesterday. This time Adele is motivated to say, "Yes, I do eat vegetables for dinner, brussel sprouts or baby peas, sometimes carrots and beans. But, no, I do not go out with runs in my pantyhose — see?" Adele shakes the plastic bag at Old Granny, timidly looking down at Old Granny's sewing basket as if her actions have nothing to do with her words. When she looks up she realizes Old Granny is asleep anyway, has fallen asleep still suspecting. Old Granny never hears what Adele has to say for herself. (All this determines that on afternoons, when other little girls drink cola and watch cartoons, Adele will read varicolored fairy tale books, sip tea and decide that the only thing she likes about sewing is the thimble. Her mother's thimble is made of mother o'pearl and silver, and quite likely is magical, because metal things worn on fingers have mysterious powers. Anyone could guess that just like her mother's ring, a thimble's magic does a lot more than protect a finger from a needle — and no one ever said you had to sew to possess one.)

But villagers are jealous of those who don't pay dues.

Adele searches her tea cup for a vocabulary. She sees the single straight tea leaf near the rim — a stick, an axe or a tree; a needle in Old Granny or the tall dark stranger that visited for a night; possibly the letter "I" but more probably a thigh bone; finally, and perhaps, all of them at once. This leads her, once again, to the thought that she has a wonderful life. Indeed, life is wonderful because she drinks Earl Grey tea. (Life is wonderful because her name sounds like the name of a princess on a chocolate box.) But outside her window a tall dark tree is shedding disconnected Latin letters like leaves, and as Adele sees them falling on Old Granny's shawl, the words remind her that she is passive and foreign. (In her little red taffeta party dress, Adele joins hands with another little girl in a yellow dress, but of like ruffles and pearly buttons; on her left side her hand is held by a blue-dressed girl. She doesn't like the blue girl, because the hand is sweaty and the dress chocolate-streaked. Round and round they go, nine or ten girls in all, and all, almost at once, fall down. They get up and do it over again. Adele holds the blue girl's hand with a minimum pressure, hoping it will slide out and that, the next time they fall, she can trade places and hold a different hand. But the blue girl likes her and follows her everywhere — until there is a call of "ice cream and cake" by a mother, whereupon a voluminous swirl of color and fabric leaves Adele abandoned on the ground.)

On fair day, sometimes she thought she heard the villagers whisper.

One day the wind is blowing hard, howling and throwing itself at the windows like winter-starved wolves. Without fail the windows will break. But Adele has already tied everything down to the bedposts — secured the bookshelves, the chairs, the lamp and the dresser drawers with the parcel string from pantyhose packages store managers leave on her doorstop. The bulbs may shatter. The books may be torn, tossed, scattered across village and forest, the clothes may be sucked up and blown until they catch, in indecent or incongruent positions, onto lamp posts, mail boxes, fire hydrants and spruce trees, but Adele feels no anxiety because she has already thrown away her underwear. Besides that, Adele is primarily interested in frames — defined, but empty spaces — which is also why she is thin, and why she does not avoid looking into the mirror. She lies down in the middle of the bed and waits. Perhaps, she thinks, the wind is persistent enough to fill her up like a balloon and carry her off. There are no remaining parcel strings with which to tie herself to the bed in any case, so she closes her eyes, determined to ignore the furious bang-bang, the inevitable break.

Hearing the urgent ding-dong, ding-dong of the bell, the villagers rushed to gather at the church. It was just as they always suspected.

The windows broke and the wind came in tearing at her, entering her, filling her as with right hand she clung desperately to a teacup, while holding warm in her left fist the thimble. The banging of the door, the flap-flapping of the sheets and the deep-throated howls of the wind circled Adele, round and round, and she saw falling colors which were really the many-colored covers of her books dropping to the floor with indistinguishable thuds, synchronously picked up and hurled out the windows and then suspended in the starry night for an indeterminable time because the tower bell (or the phone) never rang. Only the string-fastened furniture resisted, and the pink velour bedspread, which was pinned in place by Adele's edged, angled body, not, as might be suspected, weighed down by her bones.

By dawn only the handle remained of the teacup, and when the wind died away, leaving her panting on the bed, she was entirely uncertain of the magic of her thimble.

The morning has been blown clear and cold. Men chopping trees can be heard from the nearby woods, and Adele is woken by this morning sound which is all the sharper because of the broken windows. Naked and shivering, she gets out of bed and looks into her mirror. Now she finds that she has grown ears and paws and whiskers, and she finds she has eaten Old Granny and the little girl in the red dress: they are pummeling her from within, their voices whining, beseeching, and louder in Adele's newly sensitive ears than ever. Adele sees Old Granny's shawl lying outside her door amid a heap of withered leaves, but realistically she decides this must be a dream and she crawls back beneath the bedspread and lies passively, feeling her bones, the cold metallic thimble and the heavy mythic life in her stomach. (Shops do not sell pregnant Barbie dolls, and Adele has to stuff a cotton ball under her Barbie's dress because Suzie's Ken doll spent the night. Two hours later she realizes that Barbie's stomach isn't big enough, and she must replace the cotton ball with something larger and harder. She substitutes it with a big round agate she found on an Oregon beach the summer before. Why don't they sell pregnant Barbies if they sell Ken dolls, Adele wonders. Dolls with smaller dolls inside that you can take out and put back inside whenever you want to. And Adele wonders if this is realistic, but realistically she already knows they would never allow something that realistic.)

When Adele opens her eyes again Old Granny and the little red girl are sitting at the foot of her bed, pointing at her and laughing. Adele howls, a long, drawn out howl, a resonating Owwwooo. Who was it called the Woodsman? Now she remembers the grinning man who came brandishing scissors and waxed thread and needle; how with every snip her bones vibrated like a tree that must repeatedly absorb the momentum of the axe, chop-chop, until it falls; how each stone was stitched in like the ding-dong of a tower bell, and over again.

You could hear the villagers whisper.

Perhaps she was never pregnant. She's just hungry. Or the tea-leaves are to blame, the thousands she has swallowed have all balled up in her stomach into stones. They chatter and churn in her stomach, they twist sharply, but she cannot cast them out and meanwhile Old Granny still suspects her of a murder she never committed. Goodness knows how many times she has walked back and forth in front of Old Granny's door, stepping on all the sidewalk cracks to be sure, but making plain the heap of lies she has chosen to discard (the white plastic bags stretched like cauls over all the incongruous angles, the indecent edges). Yet despite all efforts she can't deny that every belonging she throws away is replaced immediately in her drawer by another — its lace, buttons, its hem and colors slightly altered but not substantially different, just as her stomach remains heavy although she doesn't eat.

21

(Mother may I, Mother May I. Mother, please, says Adele properly. You may: One big step, one medium step and three steps backwards, commands Jenny. Adele knows she will never get to be Mother, and she hates Jenny because she is taking advantage of the game, and because this is the only game Jenny wants to play, and even if Adele doesn't want to be Mother, unless she wants to go home and play by herself she will have to obey the rules.)

Adele had to conclude that disguises didn't work: Magic Thimble or not, Old Granny knew she was a wolf. And Old Granny was the one who sewed in stones. No Woodsman could have thought of that himself, nor have the skill for it.

Adele stuffed everything left into a plastic bag and deposited it and her thimble into Old Granny's sewing basket. But the hollow sound of her stomach still frustrated Adele because she had wolf ears. With wolf nose she sniffed the cold, clear pond from afar, and she caught her lupine reflection rippling gently on the water. Indeed, it was a fine morning for a swim! Adele let her bones draw her in, slowly, deeper down. (Here she can no longer discern whether she or the water is passive, or if one of them lies.) The villagers used to say you could find her deep in the woods, a place where the trees grow so dense light barely trickles through. Only a stranger could tell you how, all along, she suspected herself painfully; how when pulled up and out of the cold heavy water by the sound of a bell (the telephone? the tower?) Old Granny looked down to see her own face peering from the pond below. How the thimble slipped from her hand on to the pavement, ringing out like the pure, high laugh of a girl. How the villagers never discovered her until much later, because no one ever had time to visit the way they once did.

A VISIT TO PORTUGAL

While Kate was an independent girl, she was not without fear, and inclined to passivity unless given direction. During the spring of her senior year in college and because she had just received the trust her father had started for her years before, Kate decided to visit a foreign country. Her father would have wanted her to do that, she thought, smiling down at his old army compass. You see, Kate's father had died when she was a small child, and her mother had given her her father's army compass when she turned twelve. It was the only personal belonging of her father's still in existence — since over the years her mother had thrown out everything else — and Kate treasured it as a lucky charm.

"A useless drunk," was how her mother referred to him. But Kate only remembered how he kissed her and how he sang.

At the airport, Kate's mother counseled her to stay with an older woman. "An older woman will take care of you," she said.

"Yes, mother," Kate replied.

"Speak clearly, hold on to your purse and stay away from foreign men," Kate's mother shouted after her later as she boarded the plane, and that was about all.

Kate got a pretty fair deal on that round-trip ticket from New York to London, and from London decided to fly on to the Faro airport in Portugal. Why Portugal? A foreign student in her French class had told her it was beautiful and cheap and that there was nothing like the moon in Portugal. Besides, it would only cost her about eighty more American dollars to get there.

In Portugal, although unfamiliar with the native tongue, Kate understood enough from her grounding in French to walk about confidently, swinging her little crocodile purse and listening to street vendors call out over almonds and olives, grapes and sardines, the last of which you could also buy right on the beach, grilled and ready for the eating.

Kate felt free and happy and fancied nothing more was necessary to life.

But it did make Kate feel uneasy, a bit — all those men standing about with glittering eyes and nothing better to do than smoke.

As luck would have it, an old woman on the beach reached up and pulled Kate's sleeve. "Room?" she asked, nodding fiercely. "Room," she repeated and then, "food, cheap," she said and smiled, revealing a mouthful of rotten teeth that quite charmed the girl.

The room was dark and bare, with stone walls, one small window in the top left corner, a dresser, a narrow cot-size bed, and so inexpensive it was — almost beyond belief!

But as for the old woman — she had a slightly humped back and a little dog without much fur left. Perpetually hunched over and wrapped in a brown, moth-eaten shawl, the old woman scuttled quick here and quiet there — here slipping into the kitchen to pour a glass of sherry, there upstairs and back into her own room — just above Kate's — to drink it, and still at other times sidling over to the window and pretending to clean the sill when she actually just wanted a look. She spoke few words, and when she spoke she lisped, but she whistled and whistled often, a soft, uneven, fluttering whirr, and not quite, but almost as often, she would reach out to touch Kate's hair, she was so very fond of hair.

You could always find children chattering and hopping about her door, but they never came in. She looked like a witch, that old woman did, and she acted like one, too.

By way of Kate's French, the old woman's few words of English, a wristwatch and a clock, dinner time was arranged to be at eight every evening on the dot — the old woman would insist on that — and so Kate was left free to do as she pleased for the most part of the day while still being assured of a hot meal.

Often Kate took the old woman's little balding dog with her on walks, since so many men lolled about the streets waiting for something to happen. And what a beautiful silken leash it had, strong and supple, the color of wheat, indeed, just the color of Kate's hair. Besides which, walking the dog gratified the old woman, you could see that — how she would smile at Kate and show her crooked brown teeth; that smile could charm anyone to the bone.

Every evening at eight, when Kate returned, the old woman served her a lump of white cheese, some olives, a big plate of beans, a basket of bread, and wine — for one drinks wine in Portugal, not water. The meal never varied and that was fine. The only disturbing thing was, when they sat down together for a meal Kate felt so clumsy and large in her company — much too clumsy and large.

The other thing was that when Kate tried to fall asleep at night, usually around ten o'clock, and had turned off the light, she could hear quite plainly the cockroaches falling off the walls and scuttling across the floor, and in the morning often found dead ones on the windowsill, in her dresser drawers, in her shoes. If not that, what kept Kate awake was the large waterpipe which gurgled every thirty-five minutes and, between these periodic rushes, would drip somewhere beyond the wall. She waited for it like a train, that rumble — hearing it start in the distance, draw closer, traverse her room with a tremendous clatter, then pass on into the next room. And still yet, if it wasn't that, in the room above her the old woman stayed up, often into the very early morning, muttering and whistling softly — sometimes it even sounded as if someone else were in the room speaking to her — while there was always the restless scratching and thumping of the hairless dog who slept in front of Kate's door.

In fact the old woman occupied herself at night with a collection of dead beetles she obtained specimens for by way of neighborhood children brave enough to stick their fistfuls in through the door for a coin. The poor thing was herself too fragile, skeletally, to attempt the necessary outdoor excursions her husband had made, whom Kate heard all about one night after supper, the same and first night the old woman had begun pointing with a long finger to the room upstairs and bidding Kate follow her up. A small room it was, crowded with tables themselves cluttered up by jars and boxes and trays of beetles, some mounted in sets arranged by size and hung up on the walls, some with beautiful wings, green, red, yellow and blue, and of these wings, some decorated with hieroglyphic signs, and some with bright dots and crescents, but most — the pity of it — not made to fly — and yet still other beetles with horns and small tail-like protrusions, these surely the most fearsome to look at. After she had shown Kate this and shown her that, smiling all the time with those bad teeth that held such curious charm, they finally arrived at a large clay jar which secreted a big scarab eetle, shiny black. Next to it stood an ancient photograph of a dapper man with a moustache who, the old woman said, was her husband, who, the old woman said, had smuggled this beetle into Portugal from Egypt some thirty odd years before and twenty days later had never come back for supper.

She pulled it out with a pair of long pincers, put it on the table where it spun round and round in an effort to turn over, and waited for Kate to speak.

"It's a marvelous beetle," Kate said in French and nodded enough so that anyone could have taken her meaning.

Indeed, most marvelous was the fact of its still being alive after thirty years, a point Kate, just as any foreigner might, simply allowed for as an error in translation. The old woman smiled, showed her out the door and closed it behind her.

And now every night after they had eaten the beans and cheese and sucked the olives from their pits, the old woman motioned Kate up into her room to look at the scarab. No, Kate wasn't to look at the other beetles, for if she did, the old woman pushed her towards that big black jar, and it was only after Kate had recited "marvelous" more than once that she was let out of the room and left to entertain herself for the rest of the evening in her own room, damp and unfurnished and cold, with a single bulb for light to read by.

For even into her second week Kate wouldn't think twice of going out at night — there were too many of those men grouped about doorways and crouched upon stoops, chatting, smoking, waiting for women just like her to pass.

For it was a poor neighborhood where Kate had chosen to live. Still, above the moon shone beautiful as ever and untouched, in the distance loomed the dark shapes of mountains, and everywhere almond trees rustled and waters lapped gently for those who would hear.

And if not this, from her narrow window, almost level to the ground, you could look through to one opposite from which, at night, emanated a warm, hazy glow; if she focused long enough Kate could see men sitting around a wide cauldron-like pot which smoked profusely and which a small bent figure stirred and occasionally added something to with tongs.

Kate thought it was a soup kitchen.

So evenings became nights and always hard a thing it was to fall asleep in that room, yet on one such night Kate fell asleep early, to wake up in darkness darker than it usually was. Cold and coughing, she might have been in a tunnel the way the sound of herself echoed back loudly to her ears, and there was the strangest round hole of light in the ceiling, as perfect and bright as a full moon in a pitch black sky. But then a scraping sound — and now something clamping her leg, a shrill cackle, and now, there — the old woman herself, peering down at her and smiling.

Oh, but it had only been a dream, Kate realized as she found herself waking truly and all quite as it should be.

Kate rose late the next morning, well past noon, and decided to take a walk, leading the little dog behind her by its silken cord.

The sun was high, the sky clear and Kate made her way slowly towards a park on the outskirts of town, a sparsely treed but breezy place, with spots for visitors by the sides of sparkling fountains and artificial ponds. She sat down in the grass and gazed at a fountain bursting up in spurts so subtly uneven that at moments she questioned her focus. Then Kate was distracted by the birds flapping and fluttering against the water, and finding a penny in the back pocket of her jeans, finally got up and threw it in. It sank straight to the bottom and out of habit she wished.

The sun shone hot on her beautiful hair.

By and by Kate heard the sound of footsteps and there came a young man in a black suit. He seemed familiar to Kate, perhaps because of his moustache, which Kate thought made many men look similar, especially in Portugal. He was one of those lean, muscular men with dark hair, well tanned, walking with small, purposeful steps. Coal black and bright and sharp in the dry light, his eyes roved from side to side like people's do, who think they are being watched.

"You know, I know you," he said to Kate in English and took a seat on the grass beside her. His voice was warm and low, very like a honey bee's when heard from within a flower.

"Have we met?" Kate asked.

"Not formally, no," the man said with precision. "I've just been released from prison. I think I may have seen you on the street." Nothing more, but Kate wasn't afraid and straight away asked him what he had done. He shook his head from side to side several times and smiled with lips closed, the color of wine. The two sat and watched the fountain pulsing ever upwards, and falling, just as ever, down.

Kate looked at her watch and stood to go.

"Please," the man said, "don't go. You are pretty. Tell me about America."

"I'm sorry, I should go," Kate said, "I will be late for dinner."

"What?" the man demanded, and Kate repeated herself. "I don't understand," the man said. She tried once more, but lacking the quality of persistence Kate finally shrugged her shoulders and sat down once again.

The man smiled and lit a cigarette; it smelled heavy and perfumed.

"Would you like one?" he asked her. Kate did smoke occasionally. The cigarette was strong and fragrant, strange and and burnt slowly. The little dog splashed in the fountain, yapping at the birds.

It was such a beautiful evening, so warm and still.

Kate would have trusted anyone, her voice spoke without any effort of hers and without meaning, for they already knew each other as one, for the fountain rushed and rushed, for the trees whispered stay and stay, for the wings of birds fanned up and up, for in every moment was a thousand more, and the old woman's dog trotted home, dragging his leash behind him.

Such a pretty thing that leash — a shame it getting so muddy.

"Come with me," he said. "You must be hungry. I know where to go."

He led her along countless winding roads and stretching pavements, wove her in and out of children's laughs and mother's shouts, took her through alleys of the thinnest cats and by vineyards of the lushest grapes and on and on until the smell of sardines burst through the strange and aromatic smoke of his tobacco and a minute later she found herself on a bed in a bedroom for smallness and darkness you couldn't tell differently from her own at the old woman's, and which quite possibly was the very same.

He sat so close to her on that bed she could feel his breath upon her neck, and with a shock of repulsion she drew back. But then he braided her hair — how delightfully Kate's scalp tingled. And it was delightful then, too, when she felt all along her body,

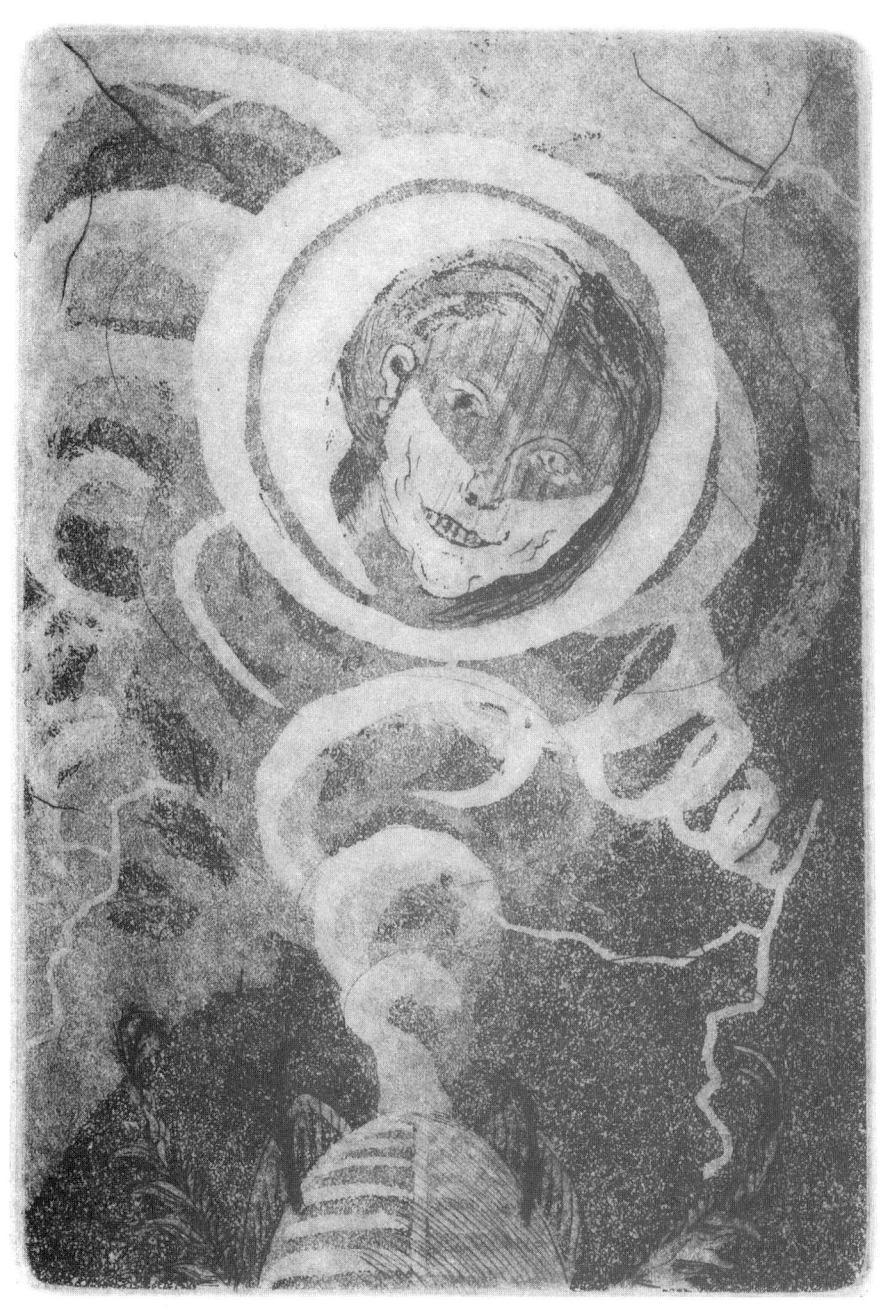

like so many little tongues clapping upon her skin, a thousand touches from a thousand directions, so soft they were only perceivable an instant as pain.

And then — if you could only see her on her back, her little legs wriggling in the air!

Pitiful thing! Lucky she doesn't know, for surely that's the only hope, although even now, once in a while, when she sees that perfect circle, that round moon of light, something grips her, something like steel, hard and cold, something like doubt spoils the charm. Because there above them, right in the middle of that marvelous light, she appears — it could be her mother, it could be the old woman, Kate can't be certain, for the teeth aren't clear enough — but to be sure someone is there, peering down and grinning, not a bit concerned for their privacy.

For those who are lucky, life seeps up from the cracks and corners with its own languorous perfume and when at last this is dispelled into the higher air, there still remains a trace to catch one's pleasure unawares. For those who have only been charmed, yes — where her father's compass spins round and round and never stops, there too might be found a duration of bliss, but it is a place second thoughts are forbidden to visit.

Oh, but when he feels her tremble, he knows what to do. He lights a cigarette, takes her in his arms, rocks her gently, sings her one of those lovely Portuguese melodies. With what hollowed sweetness his exhalations whirl back from those narrow walls! And back and back she breathes them blind, until all was a dream, was all.

And, all told, it probably takes less than a dollar a day from that little crocodile purse of hers.

EVELYN & BILL

Evelyn had chosen to work at a bank which would never run out of money, she had chosen a husband who was stable, considerate and clean, and she had chosen not to have children who would run out of the house and become accident victims. The first sign that something had gone wrong in Evelyn's life was when the habit started, a nasty physical habit. If you were lucky you could feel it start to tickle, you could push it down, keep it from getting out — but with every passing day it grew more difficult to manage.

Evelyn's husband, Bill, a dark-haired tanned man with a moustache, enjoyed downhill skiing and repairing audio components. Everyone liked Bill, and said he was a very nice man. "I love you," he shouted exuberantly to Evelyn, "it's time to get up."

"Me, too," she returned into her pillow.

When did it start? Evelyn didn't even know, you really can't remember when these horrible habits start, and all she could remember was a stuffed tiger from her childhood, with green glow-in-the-dark marble eyes. At night Evelyn used to put a pillow over his face, so she wouldn't catch him moving, his eyes circling ever nearer to her bed, animated by some unknown force of their own. But in the daytime she had loved that tiger and his tickly whiskers, and in sunlight he was the sweetest thing in the world. "Come on, honey, it's time to get up," Bill repeated.

In the winter you could smell oranges because Bill put their peels on the radiators after eating them.

Bill saw the minutest motion of a beetle scurrying under the radiator, and Evelyn heard him slap it with his slipper. She knew he heard the sheets rustle as she got out of bed. There was nothing Bill didn't miss, and this worried Evelyn, because lately she had caught herself doing it in the evenings on the couch next to her husband while they were watching television. It was luck that he hadn't seen her. Her habit was becoming increasingly compulsive.

"Put your robe on, honey. You'll catch cold," Bill reminded Evelyn.

Bill worked for the Parks Department and drove an official Chevrolet. Evelyn was a bookkeeper, and on most days it took ten minutes to walk to the bank she worked at, just downtown. When the weather was nice Evelyn and Bill met on the city hall square, a small park area with fountains, a rose garden, and plum trees, and they ate gourmet patés with french bread for lunch. In the evenings Evelyn liked to clean — she liked things to be white in her house, or shiny — and she always cooked dinner. But Evelyn depended on cookbooks for basic recipes because she didn't trust her instincts.

Bill read an article about the current fiscal crisis in Newsweek while she scrambled the eggs. Bill wanted children, and after ten years Evelyn couldn't tell him it was because she was taking pills, which she kept in her purse, confident Bill would never pry.

"Better get a move on, honey," Bill said. "You don't want to be late." Evelyn was calculating the number of shrimp needed to feed eight at the dinner party they were hosting next Saturday while she put a second coat of polish on her nails. It was eight-fifteen. She jumped up from her chair and went into the bathroom. "Will you listen to this, honey," Bill said, but Evelyn didn't hear the rest because she had turned on the water to wash her face.

Evelyn had no one to confide her troubles to. Her last best friend, Mary, had left the bank more than three years before to have a baby, and Evelyn hadn't tried to make any real friends since. Mary had told her everything, what to wear and what to do. Evelyn missed that about Mary, since she had never been able to trust mirrors and Bill always said, "You look great, honey." He put his arms around her and felt her breasts. "You're going to be late," Evelyn said. "Yeah, I guess you're right. But you better be ready when I get home!" Bill shouted from down the hall. "See you later, honey."

"Good bye! And remember to invite Lou to dinner!" Evelyn paused from brushing her teeth to shout back. Bill was so nice to her that she just couldn't face him. But he would discover the truth one of these days. She was in the red, she owed Bill, and there was nothing you could hide from him for long.

Before she left the house Evelyn called Mary to invite her to dinner. Actually Evelyn had started not to like Mary. Mary often made cruel little comments, little jabs such as, "it's lucky you have freckles, no one can tell when you break out," or, "I can't believe you really like instant coffee."

"What should I bring?" Mary asked. "Wine," Evelyn said, "white wine. We're having shrimp." "Okay, great," Mary said, "this'll finally give us a chance to catch up."

The thing was, Bill just wouldn't understand why you took pills, why you didn't want children.

Evelyn put on her coat, picked up her umbrella and her purse, checked several times to see that the stove had been turned off, and finally went out the door, locking it twice over. In the city the grays of the sky, the buildings, the streets and the wintercoats blended everything into a vague and dirty whole, and you could walk to work secure that no one held you individually responsible for anything. And while doubtless the city had its dangerous side, Evelyn felt safe because she had always put her empty deposit bottles out on the street for the poor instead of returning them or throwing them in with the trash. She always rinsed them, too, to show her respect.

Evelyn was inviting six to her dinner party. Lou, Bill's friend from work, and his wife, Jerri; Louise, from the bank, who was divorced; Frank, a neighbor; and Mark and Mary. Evelyn didn't really like Mary anymore, but Mary always called.

"We'll be a little late. The babysitter," Mary said.

Evelyn came home half an hour before Bill did. When Bill came home, they talked to each other about the people they worked with. Lou, whose Irish setter was gun-shy, should have known better than to buy from a mail-order kennel, and Louise, who breathed loudly because of sinus problems, disturbed Evelyn's ten-key rhythm.

"You look great, honey," Bill said.

This afternoon at the bank Evelyn had suddenly discovered her hand straying — in fact, she had only just caught it in time. She would have died, absolutely died! One day Bill was going to find out, Evelyn thought, setting out the napkins on the table, and that was the bottom line.

The second sign that something had gone wrong in Evelyn's life was when Mary told Evelyn about bleach. "You know, they've discovered bleach is bad for women." "Really?" Evelyn said, taking a sip of wine. "Bleach is illegal in Switzerland, you know,"

Mary said nodding. "How do you know?" Bill put in. "Oh, I forgot where I read it — but everybody knows." "Well, what exactly does it do to women?" he asked. "Oh, you know — ovarian cancer, deformed fetuses, possible sterility, that kind of thing," Mary said after swallowing a shrimp. Bill was silent. "I'm sure glad my mother never used bleach," Mary went on, "and I never have, either."

"Well my mother used bleach," Evelyn said, "and there's nothing wrong with her, or me, for that matter."

"So, Bill, how was fishing this year? Catch anything big?" Frank said.

"Nope, didn't get a chance to get up there this year," Bill shook his head.

"Remember that lake up in the Adirondacks we camped by, just after we got married? " Evelyn said. "I forgot the name. It was so beautiful and quiet," she explained, "and the water was really clear."

Everyone looked at Evelyn, the heat rose up in her face and she turned red. "That's right, honey," Bill said. It was Mary's fault, Mary who had to ruin it. Once you knew about bleach, you couldn't go back, you'd never again be able to clean your house with that same thrill of purpose. It used to make her mother so happy when she cleaned the house. Her mother came home tired, carrying a bag of groceries, but always smiled when she saw Evelyn at the sink, scrubbing at the charred patches on the frying pan.

"You know what Joshie has started to say now?" Mary said and Evelyn realized that it might have been happening right there in front of her guests while she had been thinking about her mother and the coffee stains in the kitchen sink. In the haziness brought on by the wine, Evelyn tightened her fingers firmly around the stem of the water glass.

"You know what Joshie has started to say now?" Mary repeated. "Oh, sorry, what?" Evelyn said. It was like driving across the country all night and blinking and realizing you've fallen asleep for a couple of seconds or longer because the headlights of the car on the other lane are there like two frightful bright eyes about to pounce. "He says, 'I don't remember.' Isn't that cute? I mean, most kids will say, 'I forgot,' but Joshie's saying 'I don't remember'!"

"He'll make a fine president some day," Frank said.

"I lost my job," Bill said to Evelyn when she woke up. The summer before Bill gave chlorine meant for public pools to his friends. Everyone was sorry he had been caught. It had only happened to Bill because he was always in line to do the next guy a favor, and in her heart Evelyn knew his mistake wouldn't even accounts. And by now he had seen her, she was convinced. More than once she'd caught him in the instant of looking away, and when that happens you stop, but casually, as if you intend to be seen.

"That's okay," Evelyn said, "you can paint the house. The walls get dirty so fast here, I don't know why."

"You look great, honey," Bill said, rustling the sheets beside her.

Sometimes Evelyn didn't believe how nice Bill was. Bill had probably told Lou, even Mary, all about her problem — just because Bill wouldn't want to keep secrets from his friends.

Evelyn fanned her nails dry, and then she rinsed the deposit bottles and clanked them down on the counter loudly. "Honey," Bill called, "aren't you going to give me a kiss goodbye?" But she shut the door quickly so that Bill couldn't get a look at what she was wearing, in case for once he found a fault, because once he found a fault she was certain the rest of it would spill.

Ever since Evelyn had been witnessed in the cashier's line at the neighborhood supermarket, out of embarrassment she drove to a store twenty minutes away, but in the car she realized she had forgotten her purse and overtaken by panic U-turned over the highway meridian.

Bill painted the house, and then he worked on radios.

When she got home Evelyn pinned as well as buttoned her purse so that it couldn't fall open accidentally, and she told Bill she was keeping the aspirin in the bathroom cabinet now, so he wouldn't search in her purse for it when he had a headache and when Evelyn wasn't there. She just didn't want Bill to get hurt, he was so nice, and she knew he wouldn't understand.

"Catch," Bill said, throwing her an orange tennis ball. "Hey, why don't you come with me today, honey?"

Then there were moments on weekends, especially mid-morning, when everything was so gloriously white inside! When Evelyn felt pure and peaceful amidst the freshly-painted white walls of her house, distinct from the dirty city, allowed to be her-self.

"Honey?"

"Can't. I have to clean the house, honey. You know that," Evelyn said, barely controlling her excitement at being granted a few hours of continuous indulgence, hours upon hours to be spent without fear of being caught. To be sure, letting it out for these longer periods made it stronger, reinforced your habit, but you couldn't help yourself.

Evelyn twisted the brocade button on the couch this way,

then that. Looking up she saw a hairy long-legged bug skip across the ceiling.

Still, Bill was at home every day of the week fiddling with his delicate wires and small pill-colored condensers while Evelyn tapped figures out on her ten-key at work, keeping her hands busy because she would rather die than face public exposure, and by the time the leaves fell and the radiators clunked and hissed, Bill had taken over the corner of every room, his audio parts scattered on every table, cluttering up the clear surfaces that had soothed her. Bill was in the corner of her eye, he was an inkspot on her blouse, he was a bit of spinach on the butter, never making a noise exactly, not intending to bother you, but there all the same, like the smell of orange peel, making you feel guilty the whole day long. Evelyn could never count on a moment to herself, while every moment she was anxious that Bill would suddenly say, "I saw you, Evelyn. I know."

Could she have calculated that the phone would wake her up and a man would say, "I'm sorry, Ma'am, your husband's been killed," perhaps it would have all been different, but the avalanche that buried Bill on the second day of the ski trip he'd made with a couple of friends was beyond Evelyn's control.

Bill, of course, carried a donor card, and all of his usable organs had gone to St. Luke's for redistribution. He had died of asphyxiation, and his body, more preserved by the snow than damaged, had yielded up most of its parts in perfect condition.

"Just like Bill — always wanting to do the next guy a good turn, always helping people out however he could," Mary consoled Evelyn.

"Yes," Evelyn said, "that's true," and twisting on the chair to put the phone back on the hook she pulled a muscle in her lower back.

After Evelyn collected all the bits and pieces of cassette decks, receivers, and turntables Bill had been working on in paper bags, she made a cup of coffee and called Lou, Frank, Steve and Pete to see if they wanted anything back. Then she put everything out on the street for the poor people and lay on the couch knowing Bill's insurance would provide for her. But when Evelyn fell asleep something with its own gravity, much like a large marble, began to grow at the base of her spine.

Evelyn shut her eyes and soaked in minutes of noon-time sun. Even now she could feel it gaining in density, although it didn't hurt. Mary popped off the cover of her yogurt container.

Could she have known, and now in her sudden freedom, dishes piled up in the sink, strands of spiderweb collected on the ceiling, and she wore pairs of pantyhose over and over, without washing them, until they ran.

"Bug!" Joshua shouted with excitement. "Buggie!" Evelyn opened her eyes and shaded them to see. The thing felt so heavy, that all she desired was to be horizontal. And the other was already beyond a question of control. Her job was a pretense to maintain ties to the world she no longer felt. All Evelyn wanted was solitude.

"This city is a real junkyard, you know?" Mary said. "How can you eat lunch out here, Evelyn? What do we pay our taxes for, anyway? And the school system sucks."

Could she have known, but now the milk soured in the refrigerator, the oranges softened and molded, coffee cups collected on the table, and Evelyn ate only peanut butter and jelly sandwiches.

Evelyn rolled up her paper bag, "Yes, you're right, Mary,"

she said.

"It was nice meeting you here, Evie. Start wearing a hat, or your freckles will get dark." Evelyn waved back at Mary, and just as she finished waving the impulse leapt out of the blue into her hand and brought it down to her lap with magnetic force. Evelyn automatically bent over to hide herself, but she had already been seen.

"How's it going?" a man leaning against the no-parking sign on the corner said, staring at Evelyn candidly and sucking the pulp from an orange. He wiped his mouth on his sleeve and spat a seed on the sidewalk. With the movement of her turning the weight at the base of Evelyn's back rolled and settled like a heavy ball of lead. "Fine day, fine woman," he said, nodding.

"Are those your eyes?" Evelyn asked, without surprise.

"Eyes for you, baby," he said.

"You see, Bill's dead," Evelyn began to explain, "Bill donated his eyes away," she went on. "Maybe that's why you have them — you have Bill's eyes."

"I don't know no Bill, but I guess maybe I owe the guy thanks for looking at you one way or another, honey. Right, baby?" the man laughed and winked. "Come with me," he said, taking Evelyn's arm and leading her out of the sun and the heat of the square.

"But I've really got to get going," Evelyn rehearsed, "I'll be late."

"Not too late," he said, continuing with her towards a shady alley between two large granite buildings. Everywhere Evelyn saw people peeling off, turning into offices, closing doors behind them. Lunch hour was over, and suddenly the thing was getting heavier with every second and Evelyn thought she would drop with the weight. When they reached the alley, the man pushed her and Evelyn toppled to the ground like a bowling pin.

At the beginning Evelyn felt pain at the back of her head as well as in her kidneys. Then Bill's eyes sucked her own up into them, and you could feel the very marrow of your brain being drawn out and a rushing sound filling your ears and a whiteness spreading across your vision and pooling into a great silver oval, into a peaceful, moonlit lake, bordered by forests of pine, which you could run to and jump in and swim across, your limbs pushing against the water pleasurably, until finally you rolled over on your back and floated. In the strip of sky above twin stars came out and burned down hotly, and brightly enough to make the walls gleam like white marble. At first she was afraid, for there was nowhere she could hide from Bill's eyes, but after a while Evelyn simply turned her head and gazed at her hand. The nail polish on her forefinger had chipped and all her fingers were curled in towards her palm in a relaxed grip.

The man stood up, zippered his jeans and spilled her purse out on to the pavement. After he kicked through her things to find what he wanted, he winked. "Catch you later, baby."

"Good-bye, honey," she said, except he'd already gone too far to hear.

FAMILY AFFAIR

In the summer her friends have all gone away on vacation, but Eglantine attends Everton Community College, where through a special pre-college enrichment program she is enrolled in Art History II.

"Darling, pick up some cola for me on the way home, would you," Aunt Polly says, giving her a five dollar bill.

In the summer Pauline stays in her room sewing silk ties and reading novels and drinking cola. Every fall Aunt Polly takes her ties to the arts and crafts fair downtown and always manages to sell a few, but most of them collect in boxes in the basement. Daddy lets his sister live with them.

"Remember to put some gas in the car, Eg," Mother shouts.

"I need a credit card," Eglantine says.

Gertrude goes about the house without her clothes in the summer. Of course, she's jealous of Pauline and all the ties she makes for Daddy. But Mother cooks well.

Eglantine has to turn the key once, twice before the car starts. Maybe the spark plugs, she thinks.

In the summer, as always, Daddy works a forty-hour week as a civil engineer. From the window, you can see the impressive Everton Dam that he helped design. A sketch of the dam that Eglantine made in her high school 2D class also hangs over the sofa.

Evenings, just minutes before Daddy comes home carrying

the Everton Tribune in one hand and fingering his short brown moustache with the other, Mother remembers to put on a lacy black robe and pours him a glass of seltzer, because Daddy doesn't drink anymore.

"What's for dinner, Mother?" he says, loosening his tie and withdrawing his reading specs from a pocket to read the paper.

"Why did I ever marry him?" Gertrude declares, yet she seems to draw some sort of satisfaction from serving dinners to Daddy, dinners which she prepares with an eye first to color combination and only second to nutritional value. Gertrude was an art major herself when she went to college, and has always encouraged Eglantine to pursue her talent.

Eglantine gets home from class before Daddy gets home from work, and most of the time lies in bed chewing the nail on her index finger. Always the quiet, unobtrusive type, she mostly stays in her room and sketches nature scenes; she could go outside, but it's more depressing there. The house was a new house when the family moved in and now, even after two years, no grass, shrubs, flowers or trees have been planted; meanwhile, time keeps creeping along, measured in nerve-wracking intervals by bursts from Aunt Polly's sewing machine in the next room. A wave of hopelessness descends upon Eglantine. The distant hum of the Pacific in her seashells.

On summer nights, if Eglantine can fall asleep, she dreams of vast, verdant gardens, but more often she watches the door, and in the dim aura of her Mickey Mouse night-light the doorknob and its shadow loom out at her, a protruding bulbous eye and its darker, larger double.

Daddy knocks and opens the door a crack. "Good night, Princess — and sweetest dreams."

Towards the end of June, there's a knock at the front door. Gertrude slips on her black lacy robe and lets in a short, sturdy man in a light blue shirt and jeans, carrying a metal tool box. His name is Claude, and he is an auto mechanic and sculptor Gertrude met at the local Gas Up! station last spring. Gertrude has invited him to set up a studio in the basement.

Of course, in fact they are contriving to murder Daddy, to marry and move to The Village.

Mother bares her breasts and Claude nibbles them in the foyer. She can hear Mother giggle. Claude moves into the basement well before Daddy arrives home and the day proceeds insensible of change. But this night of all nights Eglantine dreams Daddy is stalking up and down the hall and pausing to rattle her doorknob and moan, "Help me. Help me, me before it's too late."

Daddy is quite composed the next morning at breakfast, however, drinking a cup of good strong French coffee and eating grape jelly and peanut butter on pita bread, his favorite combination.

"How goes the history, Princess? Any summer romances brewing?" he winks.

"Daddy," she answers smoothly, "there's an auto mechanic in the basement."

"Aha," he winks again, "so that's where my little girl hides those boyfriends of hers." But her words having succeeded in turning Mother pale. Gertrude casually spins her butter knife until it stops to point at her plate. "What an imagination you have, dear," Gertrude says.

"Still waters run deep, you know," Pauline offers through a mouthful of wheat-bran pellets, waving her spoon vaguely in the air.

"Well, I wish deep waters would run still for a change," Gertrude retorts bitterly, getting up and banging her cup down in the sink.

"Now, now girls," Daddy raises a finger genially. "If Princess imagines an auto mechanic in the basement, there he will stay. Oh, no — I'm late again," Daddy adds, shaking his head with sincerest regret. He kisses Mother's cheek and pauses a moment to let Pauline straighten his tie — a lovely paisley she gave him for Christmas — before he leaves. When Gertrude hears the BMW drive off, she instantly takes off her robe and skips downstairs to do laundry in the basement.

"What do you think, baby doll?" Claude asks Gertrude for an opinion of his work, a contemporary Aphrodite constructed from sundry auto parts. He has just set the goddess's torso into an oil pan meant to perform as an oyster shell.

"A bit too derivative," Gertrude says. She kicks one of the many boxes in the basement that store Pauline's home-sewn ties. "Maybe you can incorporate these things in one of your projects," she suggests sourly.

"C'est une merveilluse idée, ma cherie! I weel do it," Claude affects a French accent and playfully grabs one of Mother's breasts.

"Darling," Pauline calls out when she returns from Everton Community College. "Eg, darling, fetch your auntie a cola, please." Eglantine makes up a couple of saltines with peanut butter for herself before taking the cola to Pauline's room. She finds Aunt Polly reclining on her salmon satin divan smoking an Eve cigarette and thumbing through a fashion magazine.

"Darling," Aunt Polly lowers her voice to a whisper. "Something's going on down there." She nods toward the basement. "I suspect your mother is fooling around. I may be old-fashioned — still! In your father's own house!"

"It's no secret," Eglantine shrugs scornfully. "Besides, I've heard you fooling around before."

"What do you mean? You must be imagining things, dear."

"I've heard you in here with someone."

"I don't think so, dear," Aunt Polly laughs, waving her hand. "By-the-way, how do you like that brocade over there? Too stiff? Too overbearing? I'm considering trying a line in this stuff. Fashions are getting a little more decadent again, you know . . . " Pauline languidly gestures her toward the door, the affair in the basement already forgotten.

When she returns to her room she can indeed hear Mother and Claude speaking softly just below her in the basement, their voices snaking up the heating vent in the corner of her room.

"But when?" Mother is asking.

"Mais patience, baby doll. I've got everything under control," Claude reassures her and licks Mother's breast.

"Oui," Mother moans, "oui, oui, oui." Now he's biting her nipple.

Daddy comes home, pours a glass of seltzer and runs a bath. Eglantine sits very still on her lacy white bedspread and listens to the water run. Outside her window, a flapping of wings, the high squeal of an animal, but when she goes to look all is as still and dreary as ever. She drops her art history book on the floor and begins a heedless drawing of desert mountains, then puts her sketchbook aside and lies back on her bed, the familiar noises of Daddy in the bathroom lulling her until she succumbs entirely to the sensation of being pushed down into the white lacy bedspread, as if she were a vegetable seed and her mattress the earth, giving way beneath her so gradually that only the light above, shrinking to a pinpoint, alerts her of her descent. "Here I am," a voice rises to meet her and laps around her body. "Here I am, my precious." "Daddy?" She sits up abruptly and then looks down at the heating vent. "Claude?" she whispers, but she hears nothing except Aunt Polly's sewing machine starting up, starting up again.

"Dinner time," Mother calls through the door.

"Dinner time," Pauline echoes a few moments later.

"I heard, I already heard," she mutters.

Daddy's face is rosy and good-humored at the dinner table. He remarks how pretty Eglantine looks in her yellow blouse and puts a fork into the salmon to hold it down, fastidiously fishing out its cheeks with a knife. Outside, just at the left of the dining room window, the dam gleams impassively beneath the pinkening sky and vacationers in mini-vans and RVs rush along the highway to make good time.

Alongside the salmon Mother has served white boiled potatoes and blueberries and wears a tight-fitting red-striped sundress. The eating implements chink against the porcelain and the force of gravity increases in proportion to the humidity.

"Well," Daddy smiles, mopping his neck with one of the linen dinner napkins, "Sometimes I really have to say to myself: Energy conservation be damned, we need an air-conditioner."

"All this humidity is good for your skin, though," Pauline says.

"Makes you feel kind of sexy, too," Gertrude adds.

Downstairs in the cooler depths of the basement Claude begins work on Aphrodite's ear by attaching a shock absorber.

Mother brings in dessert. Lime meringue pie!

"Mmm," says Daddy, "good pie, isn't it Princess?"

"Mmm," Eglantine agrees obediently, but as she reaches for another piece she knocks over Daddy's seltzer glass, and it rolls off the table and shatters on the floor.   For a second, they all freeze perfectly still.

At 4 a.m. the next morning, Eglantine goes outside to look at the moon, low and full and blurry in the humid air, and a car without a muffler drones along the highway. She attaches the hose Daddy bought last month to the faucet. The moon is pink and weepy, like a conjunctive eye, and as the water begins to splash out from the hose there is a prolonged, mournful "whoo, whoo," of an owl invisibly perched somewhere in the neighbor's yard. Eglantine concentrates intently as she waters the yard, waves the hose to make snaky curves and spiralling alphabets on the cement-like crust of earth that, due to her routine early-morning dousings, is actually quite porous underneath, grown more receptive, ready for planting. She waters for almost an hour, then returns to her bedroom, just before the morning birds begin to chirp, sing, search for worms.   Again a peaceful floating sensation surrounds her until she falls into a dream and a heavy, masculine body takes its place, lying on top of her, breathing hotly into her face.

Sometime after Daddy has left for work she is woken by Aunt Polly's sewing machine. She's stumbling groggily down the hall, Aunt Polly comes out, wears silver slippers and a purple kimono that exudes patchouli, pounces. "Bad dreams?" Aunt Polly asks her. "I thought I heard you moaning and moving around in there."

"I suppose you want a Coke," Eglantine replies.

"How long have you actually been with Gas Up! Claude?" Gertrude asks him as they come upstairs to get a bite for lunch.

"Well, let's see. Twelve, almost thirteen years now, baby doll. How about that? Owww! Jeeze, it's a piece of glass." Claude hops to the dining table and picks a tiny shard out of his foot just as Eglantine comes into the kitchen.

"Oh," Eglantine says. "Thought I got it all. Broke a glass last night."

"That's okay," Claude reassures her generously, "No real harm done." Gertrude leads him to the dining room table and when he sits down, kneels to suck the wound on his foot. Claude gathers her long blonde hair and twists it in a knot at the top of her head, exposing her neck. Holding her hair with one hand, he takes a Swiss Army knife from his pocket and shaves the downy hairs of the nape with the other.

"Oh, Claude, don't. Don't, baby, you're giving me goose bumps," Gertrude protests, wriggling away and getting up on his lap. "Anyway, as I was going to say, Claude," she attempts again, seriously. "You should see about getting Gas Up! mechanics unionized."

"Good idea," Claude nods his head thoughtfully. "So, kid" he addresses Eglantine, "How do you like the way things are working out? Just like we planned, huh."

"Guess so."

"You frightened me when you told Daddy, dear," Gertrude says. "You really shouldn't tease me like that. You do want to go to New York with us don't you, Eg?" Gertrude threatens feebly, smiling up at Claude and toying with the chest hair that peeks from his shirt.

"Don't worry Mother, nothing will go wrong," Eglantine sighs.

"Wait a minute," Gertrude says, staying Claude's hand

which had been on its way up her thigh, "I want to put on those
pretty lace-up gloves you gave me."

Mother leaves the room and Claude eats a saltine.
"Tonight," he says quietly when Mother's out of earshot. "We'll do
it ce soir, baby, " he touches her and then sniffs his fingers.
"You're some little girl." Mother returns wearing a long black lace
up glove on her left arm and drawing another up her right. "Tie it
for me, lover boy," she giggles, offering her arm. The kettle whistles and Eglantine quickly walks past it and out the door all the
way to the garage where she can finally laugh out loud.

The plan is a cinch. She will mix arsenic in his seltzer, will
offer it to him, he will drink it, she will run a bath for him, he will
get in and, depending on what option they go for, they will make
it look as if he has drowned in the bathtub. They say it happens all
the time.

Eglantine is rolling open the garage door with a vigorous
flourish when suddenly a huge owl swoops out at her, wings just
brushing the top of her head, startles her into a moment of fear,
even remorse about what's going to be done. But by the time she's
turning the key she's back imagining all the fun she'll have with
Mother.

"There you are," Aunt Polly calls from her room. "Be a darling and fetch me a cola, would you." Routinely, Eglantine eats
crackers with peanut butter, brings the bottle of Coke to Pauline.

Downstairs in the basement, Gertrude hangs from a water
pipe, her arms knotted to the pipe with ropes made from Pauline's
silk ties, which have been twisted together for extra strength.
Other than the belt from her robe, which Claude has arranged
loosely around her waist, she is naked. Her nipples have little

tooth mark rings around them. The dryer buzzes.

"There you are," Gertrude says as she descends the steps, "How was class? Eg dear, would you be a good girl and take those out and fold them for me." Opens the dryer door, starts folding Daddy's shirts while Claude slides under Mother's feet to insert large nuts and bolts between her toes. "I'm getting a bit tired, Claude," Gertrude says, pulling herself up a little so that the ties don't chafe at her wrists. "I don't think I'll have the stamina for this live installation thing after all. Have you ever thought about video?"

Reaches up, puts one of the lace-up gloves Mother left on the washer into her mother's mouth, leaving the laces to dangle flirtatiously. Picks up a stack of pee-colored Everton Tribs, arranges them beneath her mother's feet.

"Let's get started. Not much time."

"Your wish is my command," Claude says, wetly kissing her palm.

"I think we should try to do a single medium thing. Emphasize the flesh quality," Eglantine says. Steps back, squints her eyes, steps forward, unbraids Mother's hair. Gertrude kicks, flaps, mute as a fish, but taking Eglantine's suggestion to heart, Claude pinches up and down her legs and abdomen with pliers, creating large leopard-like blotches of red. Eglantine folds out Claude's Swiss Army knife and slits a long "S" shape from just above the left breast to the umbilical knot. Carves in a few confetti-like squiggles on the right breast to suggest "fun". Blood patters on the newspaper, Mother faints, head lolls to the right side.

"Hmm," Eglantine ponders the effect this has had on her original conception. "Incorporating the random, that's what it's all about, " she comments to Claude, saws at the ties around Mother's right wrist until that arm falls free. Steps back, squints at her work. "Almost there." Steps forward again to slash the main artery on the underside of Mother's left arm, rips firmly through the skin and vein down the forearm from the wrist, the frisson of tearing, finishes off with precisely nicked cross-hatches that create a fleshy double for the actual glove to be laced up Mother's right arm.

"Oui, oui, oui!" Claude exclaims with enthusiasm. "It's too bad we can't show her somewhere."

"Wait," Eglantine says, undoes the belt around her mother's waist. Panting a little from the effort, drags a stool over and climbs up to make a Minnie Mouse-like bow around her mother's hair. "There. You know, knowing when to stop is the true test for the artist, Claude."

Both of them stand back for a moment to admire their creation in silence, then Claude pinches Eglantine's cheek and starts gathering up his tools. He picks out one of Aunt Polly's ties from a box and knots it loosely around his neck. "N'est-ce pas?" he grins. The tie is patterned with yellow poodles strutting at the foot of the Eiffel Tower.

It's hot. Mother's dead, and Aunt Polly's busy sewing, her machine buzzing every thirty seconds or so. In the kitchen Eglantine pours Claude a bubbling glass of seltzer and together they nibble at saltines and peanut butter until Daddy gets home.

"Come sit on your Uncle Claude's lap," Claude pats his knee, and Eglantine acquiesces obediently. "Okay, now for the hard part," he continues, "But even that will be easy, n'est-ce pas?" Claude grins, taking another sip of seltzer. "After all," he resumes, "With your mother's history nobody will think twice about her running off and your father's suicide would be natural, right? Everybody knows how much he loved your mother — and he wasn't Catholic, was he?" She shakes her head. "Well Uncle Claude is here. He'll take care of his little girl for a couple of years. . ." He unbuttons her yellow blouse and squeezes her breast suggestively.

"I feel so sticky. You know, we could take a bath before Daddy gets home," Eglantine proposes.

Claude tilts his head like a parrot.

Starts the bath, Claude brings his seltzer with him, gets in. Finally, convulsions, he slips down into the water, bubbles rise up from his nose and mouth to the surface, disappear. Daddy pulls up in the driveway.

"Did everything go as planned?" Daddy comes in the door and peers at the dead Gas Up! mechanic good-naturedly. He takes out his spectacles from his shirt pocket with his right hand and fingers his moustache with the other. "He was an exceptionally hairy man, wasn't he?"

They eat an omelette for dinner and when it's dark drag Claude into the backyard. Daddy shovels several feet down into the patch of earth Eglantine watered the morning before, they roll Claude's body in, toss his tool box, jeans and light-blue shirt after.

In the basement Daddy sighs as they look at Mother. "So? What do you think?" she asks, unable to restrain her desire for feedback.

"What can I say, Princess? I guess we were married too long."

She frowns, "No, Daddy. I mean my work, how do you like my work?"

"Oh, I'm sorry, Princess — just not all here, today. It's fine. Excellent. Yes, a masterpiece," he pauses and pats her on the head. "Here, help me get her down." When they get Mother upstairs and outside, they roll her in on top of Claude. "Tell you what," Daddy pants, "I know how much you've been wanting it, and tomorrow I promise I'll make an appointment with Chem-Lawn."

"Oh, Daddy!"

Daddy looks toward the dam. The wind is picking up, overpowering the other night sounds, and the thunderstorm is closing in; for a moment, the dam gleams like a shiny hubcap, but then the moon is gone. "A wonder of civil engineering," Daddy says, almost regretfully. He goes inside to call the Everton police and report Mother missing, as well as his suspicions that she may have gone to New York with a Gas Up! auto mechanic named Claude.

"I'm sorry, sir, we can't interfere in domestic affairs unless there's actual violence. Let us know if you hear anything more specific," the police officer says predictably.

"Why don't you go to your room for awhile," Daddy says. "I've got to let Aunt Polly know what the deal is."

Lying on her bed she hears Daddy's voice mumbling in Aunt Polly's room, hears Aunt Polly's giddy giggles, cannot make out entire phrases because the irritating buzz of the sewing machine keeps on. She knows what's going on, always has. Keeps on. Only a few minutes more. Stays awake, chews her finger, concentrates on the doorknob. Whispers softly to it: "You're just a mutant mushroom/ looming in the night/leering in the light/of Mickey Mouse!" "Whoo, whoo," screeches owl. But Auntie's sewing machine won't say; it's the motor of Daddy's BMW purr, purr, purring. Away!

Eglantine opens the front door, the headlights of

Daddy's car slash across the whites of her eyes cinematically. As it reverses down the driveway she glimpses the silhouette of Aunt Polly's arm raising a cola bottle — or she pulling through some hand-sewing thread with a needle? Daddy's looking straight ahead, but his hand slips from Pauline's thigh for a moment to shift into first.

Eglantine dances in the dim, pink light of the emerging dawn. Yes, she loved him, but a new sense of freedom rushes over her all at once, as if Daddy's dam had split at the seams and swept her into the world.

13

Displaying all the signs of having been built at least one Southern Californian decade earlier, the walls of the Islander were white with pink and aqua colored bricks set in diamond patterns along the top, above which skinny-necked palms could be seen straining inwards. A desert palace, she might imagine. But she had never been inside, and when she passed the shouts and splashing heard from within betrayed a different reality. The very idea of the tanned pubescent bodies secreted within, their electric shades of swimsuit, repulsed her, and she had heard children speak of having seen other children urinate in the pool. Daily she walked by the Islander to get to the horse stables, daily its portals disclosed beach party teens acting in some perpetual, flirty toothpaste commercial.

She was not one of them. First, her pale, red-head's skin made her feel like a freak. Then, they could only be despised, with their happy, healthy sun-glow bodies that thought the world was fine. She wanted to dissolve in the rain that never rained in California, she wanted to disappear in the shadows, to spring from the dark at them and slash their faces.

Of course, she did want a boyfriend, and boys were interested in revelation. Boys did not have time to discover secrets. She especially liked anti-social boys with discipline problems and dark hair. She liked the way they refused authority, the way they smoked out under the abandoned overpass behind the school, the way they wore discarded army jackets. She wanted to learn from them how to be bad. It was really a very stereotypical situation she found herself in, and who's to say that it wouldn't have been different growing up in Oregon, where the seasons were rainier and the pines thick with places to disappear. Who's to say she wouldn't have been planning even now to run away to Southern California, if she hadn't been there already?

She wanted boys that crawled out from under the rocks, from behind doors, and the only rule was not to take yourself seriously.

The particular boy was her friend Becca's brother. She had witnessed him with older girls in halter tops, driving them around on the proverbial motorcycle, revving at the corners. Sometimes he'd appear at the stables, where Becca had a horse, and he'd joke around with her and her friends because he was drunk and bored. Becca told her he was on parole from having stolen guns from his uncle, and he had been kicked out of high school after hitting his history teacher with his own ruler. When she slept over at Becca's she'd stay up watching t.v. until he came home from whatever party he'd been at. He'd smoke a joint with her sometimes. His name was James.

Her parents: were there parents? She had never done anything wrong in her life, anyway, so their existence wasn't of significance.

Staying over at Becca's on the weekends, she get up two or three hours after James went to bed, to help Becca and Rhonda with the paper route. It was a ruse — they all knew — it was a trade. No conscience necessary. She got to hang around James if she helped Becca. Becca herself was getting to be a drag. Becca was attracted to nice boys with pimples, or gawky FFA rednecks. And yet her brothers were so cool. Becca's friend Rhonda was a deaf girl, and they'd do a tedious sign language routine every morning before the route, drinking coffee. Rhonda had frizzy hair, bad acne, and had slept with both of Becca's brothers. Once Rhonda took her aside and in her thick, furry voice tried to warn her how nasty Becca's brothers were. Rhonda was strong, her grip on her shoulder hurt; she worked at the stables, helped break horses. She wanted to shake Rhonda off, Rhonda only elicited her pity; she wanted to laugh and say, "I know," but she had to admit it was a moment of compassion on Rhonda's part. Rhonda was actually trying to protect her from Becca's brothers! Poor deaf girl, the kind of girl who got used because she wasn't cute enough to keep. Well, if you were going to play, you couldn't expect anybody to play by rules. Rules for girls were boring anyway. Who really wanted to go steady, get trotted around by one guy all the time?

Those early morning paper routes actually had a lyric quality. Silence, darkness, being privy to glimpses of the rich in their lighted kitchens and living rooms. Becca spared her nothing. They started on the route at 5:30 in the morning, each setting out in a different direction. Inevitably she was given the hill, because it was a bitch to do. But in the cool hours of the morning, it seemed to grant her secret access to the everyday lives of the rich. Having the right to walk up to their doors in the early dawn, looking into their windows, seeing the women get up to make coffee, the men knotting their ties. It crossed her mind to use her knowledge of these lives — maybe let James know who was worth breaking into, and when the houses were empty.

The crows collecting and cawing, streetlights clicking off, whirly-bird sprinklers beginning to tick-tick-tick and hiss, doors opening behind her as people picked up their papers, the smog still visible as a settled ribbon along the mountains to the east that, by afternoon, would already be indistinguishable from the general haze of the sky. The palms were utterly still. There was only wind here, never breezes. But here, at this time of morning, she was a ghost, no one questioning her presence or absence; this was the time she could be left outside of life, a voyeur.

Every third house on every block had a pool. Rhonda had a pool, but her parents didn't let anyone but family use it. There it was, just over the fence behind Becca's house. She'd seen Rhonda diving in it. She was strong and tan, so tan her teeth gleamed out at you. She was like a powerful animal, swimming.
It would have been nice to have your own pool.

The stables were at the foot of the hills, more like barren rocky heaps, full of lizards and snakes and gopher holes to startle the horses that actually none of them rode very often. Mostly they sat on the alfalfa bales under the rain shelter, chewing alfalfa straws and talking ninth grade. The flies and the sweat and the dust; the smell of leather, hay and horse manure. The horses snorting and stamping in their 15 x 20 pens, whinnying for oats. Mini-bikes whining on the hills in the distance. The door of the tack shed creaked, and Rhonda came out with a saddle and bridle. Rhonda was working with Becca's Morgan, a stubborn 5 year old gelding. Punching him on the neck with her fist to stand still and shouting at him in her muffled, deaf-girl voice, she buckled on the saddle. That was her problem, why she wasn't good with her own horse the way Rhonda was. She wasn't brave enough to be boss; horses seemed too big and powerful to even begin to pretend to order them around. She offered Becca a cigarette.

Later, Becca's brother James showed up at the stables on his motorcycle, drunk. He leaned back on the seat, closing his eyes in the sun. What an idiot, Becca sneered, out of earshot. After awhile he sat up and yelled, Hey, can I ride your horse. No, she answered, I'm going home, James. C'mon Rhonda. How about your friend? She have a horse? he persisted.

She was scared to death riding on his motorcycle, but thrilled. Lean with the turns, he told her. She leaned with him further than he did, looking down at the asphalt almost touching it, trying not to squeeze his waist too hard. They got to the park. A couple of swans skimming the pond; green trees and grass and shade, and not a soul around. Hey, James said, peering into her eyes groggily. I don't know, she said. He stuck his tongue in her mouth. She wasn't sure yet if the appropriate response to this was to stick your tongue back in his mouth. Come on, he said. She unbuttoned her denim shirt, pulled off her t-shirt, and took off her jeans and her panties under the blanket. Jeeze, you're tight, he said. I've never done it before. Oh, great, you're a virgin. I'm sorry, she said, I guess I should've told you. I can't believe it, you're a fucking virgin.

An old woman with a Bullock's shopping bag walked past them. James laughed. What are you looking at you ancient fucking vegetable? She looked away at the pond. She was going to die. She tugged the blanket up around her.

James offered her a Marlboro red. So, you're my sister's friend, right? James asked, playing dumb. Yeah, that's right, I've seen you over at the house, he nodded.

It was exhilarating. On the way home, she didn't know what he was thinking, but the wind blowing their hair back, and she could hold on to him and smell the back of his shirt. Hey listen — what about tomorrow night? We could try again. Sure, she said, and her heart was filled with joy.

Set the table, her mother said when she walked in the door, and she knew she'd made it home in time.

She'd always been the best in the class up until now. Maybe it was because the chalkboard was a lot further away, and she refused to wear her glasses. But she couldn't understand this old bald guy either. He spoke a lot faster than Mademoiselle Dauphin in Middle School, where she and Becca had memorized all the lessons, and could repeat them to each other on horseback. Bonjour, Marie. Allo, Monique. Comment allez-vous? Bien merci, et vous? Ca va. Aimez-vous le professeur d'histoire? Oui, il est beau, n'est-ce pas? Oh, ouiii! Not this guy. And he pointed at you, he picked you out of nowhere, in front of all those other kids, all those rich soc types she had never seen before. She was the only one who wore a denim shirt and smoked. The rest of them still ate Twinkies and wore braces. She was the only cool one there, and they were morons. Becca hadn't signed up for French this time, she was raising a lamb for the Ag class. Well, she was going to drop tomorrow. She wouldn't wear shoes to class. Je n'accepte jamais les pieds nus dans ma classe, he would say. C'est domage, c'est fromage, she would shrug and walk out. That was it. Forget fucking French, who ever met any French people anyway.

Hey, you still have the same shirt on, James said. Smells like a fucking horse. She shrugged, this was her coolest t-shirt, her blue tie-died t-shirt. Do you ever change clothes? Do you shower? he said sarcastically. Yes. Well, get on, let's go. He took her up into the hills this time. They rode over the railroad tracks, and she was sure they'd die. But the moon was full, and the landscape was illuminated enough to see the path. They got to the top of the hill. Let's get high, he said, and stopped. They sat on the large flat rocks and gazed down while they passed the joint. Silence. Stars. Nice. Beneath them was the Islander, the eerie turquoise glow of the pool. She saw how large it was, the space inside the walls. Hey, I wonder if Hans is down there, James said. Who? Hans Krueger — See, over in the corner, down by those oleanders? There was a whole group of kids gathered in the shadows, the little flickers from their cigarettes flaring as they took hits; but in fact she saw nothing but the vague outlines of volleyball net poles and the ever-present palms outlined in the night sky. I didn't know people went in there at night. Yeah, I usually get my lids from Hans. It's not too bad, huh? he asked, nodding at the joint. She could never be sure if James was joking or not, and she hadn't the slightest idea. Mmm, she nodded. So — anyway, how do you get in? What? The Islander? Oh, you can get over the walls, James said. It's easy. He stubbed out the roach and put it in his pocket. So, come here, he whispered. She inhaled him, looked up at stars, heard the stomp of the horses in their pens only half a mile away.

This would be the last time they could pass. She and Becca dressed like hobos and started out at nine, late enough that chances were good people would give them the rest of their candy. Trick or Treat. Here, take it all, I don't want it around the house, they remembered a fat woman saying the year before. Except for the paper route, this would be the last time she could walk around at night with a decent excuse. Trick or Treat. Aren't you too old for this?

Sorry, all out of candy, Becca's neighbor said. She just hates us, Becca said. My stupid brothers are always parking in front of her driveway, and she thinks my mom's mini-skirts are too short.

They went back to Becca's house and watched *Night of the Living Dead* on t.v. with Rhonda. When Becca fell asleep, Rhonda stayed. Becca's mom came home. Hi! she said. Having fun? Did you guys go trick-or-treating tonight? Well, don't stay up too late girls. I'm pooped. See you in the morning, she said, and she left the room flooded with Charlie cologne. Rhonda fanned the air in front of her nose and laughed. She lit a cigarette. Maybe Rhonda was waiting for James to get home, too. Rhonda said something to her, but she just couldn't understand Rhonda, and it just made it more uncomfortable. They watched a Cal Worthington and His Dog Spot commercial. Finally Rhonda got up and waved good-bye. Then she heard James' motorcycle pull up, but he didn't come in. She looked out the window and she saw him and another girl leaning against the garage door. She was older, and had longer hair, but it was brown. There seemed some comfort there.

Every night she could she sneaked out of the house, walked the mile to Becca's by cutting through people's lawns and ducking in the bushes when cars came out, in case the Hillside Strangler was stalking their area. She didn't even pretend to be "spending the night" over at Becca's anymore. She could just walk in the house, and crawl into James' bed, and sneak out in the morning after Rhonda and Becca had left to do the route. She could get in the back door and walk straight into his room. Tonight it was locked, but as usual there was the glow of the gas burners in the kitchen, left on to keep the kitchen warm. The house was never locked. Tonight it was. She waited for awhile. She was cold, she was tired. She could see James' door was closed. Maybe he was home already and fast asleep. She wanted him, she wanted to smell his tobacco breath, and hear him play Wild Horses on his guitar while he looked into her eyes, and in his little room when the door was closed, she believed he did love her, that he was just putting up a front for everybody outside. But his door was closed. The other girl might be with him for all she knew. The garage had been locked so she couldn't check if his motorcycle was there or not. Becca did this, she thought. Becca, that bitch. She couldn't climb back in her bedroom window at home — too difficult to climb in from the outside. Besides, if she were caught it would blow her usual excuse for coming home at 7:00: I went to feed Whiskey early so I could ride him later this morning, she'd say, nodding off in her cereal bowl.

Whiskey, her black gelding, snorted and stamped, having already smelled her when she came over the top of the path to the stables. She didn't have her key to Rhonda's tack shed, so she couldn't give him any oats, and it was much too early for his hay. She curled up on one of her own bales of alfalfa, and tried to sleep. The sounds of the horses stamping and snorting around her were company, but she was freezing. Just before dawn, she got up. Someone was walking up the stable road, and waved; it was a while before she realized it was Rhonda. Hi, she said. But she didn't say anything more, just cut the wire on one of her own bales and grabbed a chunk of alfalfa to give to her horse.

At dawn, she put on Whiskey's saddle-pad and bridle and galloped him around the paddock. He didn't want to run. She kicked and he galloped heavily, as if magnetized to the ground. She gave up and rode him back to his pen.

It was James's idea, of course, to go skinny dipping in Rhonda's pool. Come on, he said. But what if someone sees us? They won't. Come on! And he lead her out the back door and helped her over the fence and they slid into the pool without making a splash and she glided up and down the length of it. It was rare she got to swim, she was so self-conscious of her white, untannable skin, she didn't like being seen. The water was a pleasure, she liked the silence of swimming just under it, the ability to move on a plane. James watched her swim up and down two, three times. In the light of the pool, she felt like a blacklight poster pinned on a wall, except under a real blacklight her skin looked neat, and you couldn't tell it wasn't tan. Here she felt absolutely naked. It seemed romantic though. Unfortunately, it didn't work out, he couldn't enter her. It seemed impossible in the water, she didn't know why, perhaps the chlorine was shrinking her up, drying her like a prune. They gave up and went inside, and he didn't feel like it any more.

Rhonda took her to The Islander to buy a lid. She had saved $10 for this, and it would be her first spoken interaction with the cool high-school kids who hung out in the parking lot. There was high ground behind the back wall of the Islander, and Rhonda cupped her hands so she could scale the wall. Rhonda herself was taller, and stronger, and shimmied over without difficulty. Inside, four guys were hanging out. Hans, the dealer, nodded at her in acknowledgment. A half? She guessed so. He took a joint out, lit it, then handed it to her. She inhaled, choked, passed it around to the other guys. Rhonda was waiting in the shadows, near the wall. Hans slid a plastic bag toward her. She looked at it, and shrugged. Ten dollars? she asked casually as possible. He nodded, and she gave him the ten. Good doing business with you, man, he stubbed out the joint and politely shook her hand. Hey dudes gotta hit the road see you around. A couple of the guys left with him, one stayed back. She'd seen him around before, hanging out in James' bedroom and smoking pot. He never said a word to anyone; James made jokes about him, being friends with him just because he always had pot. Becca heard he'd been permanently freaked out on acid. Others said he was a junky. He had brown frizzy hair just like Rhonda's, except he was skinny and white as a slug. Rhonda came towards them. Smoke with me? Rhonda said, pinching her fingers up to her lips. I don't have any papers, she said. Rhonda took some out of her pocket, and smiled. The guy followed them, uninvited, to the bench where Rhonda rolled a joint.

The Islander was deserted except for them. She wandered around, still not sure if she was high, examining the baby pool attached to the big pool, the sand area laid out for volley ball, the closed-up concession stand. No great mystery after all. She wanted to see what the restrooms were like, and discovered that they were in a kind of tunneled dungeon, completely dark and sealed off from any outside light, and she couldn't find the electric switches. Inside, she made out the bathroom doors, but not the Boy and Girl signs; she distinguished the faint gleam of a urinal in the first, and as she turned to move on, realized he was behind her. She comprehended. Hey, let's go smoke some more reef, she said loudly. She tried to move back, past him, back towards the light of the pool, but he turned and pinned her to the wall. She was shocked at how strong he was, this skinny dude. He tried to kiss her, and she couldn't turn her head aside. No! Let me go, she said. He didn't say a word. She could hardly see his face. But he didn't loosen his grip, and she couldn't budge. His body pressed hard against hers. He smelled like Ivory, and briefly she pictured her mother. Let me go! she said, but her voice squeaked nothing, and salt was coming up in her mouth — she'd been taken by fear. With his left hand he fumbled with her jeans, first trying to rip them off, then feeling more precisely for a button and a zip. He got in and put his hand in her crotch, she felt his fingers inside her and involuntarily she came, it was as if something had sprung inside her. It had never happened to her before, but the way he stopped and looked at her with a kind of triumph, she knew what it was, what she'd done.

In another moment he was slammed back against the wall behind him. You bastard! Rhonda yelled. You bastard! in her fuzzy voice. Rhonda grabbed her arm and took her away, and before she knew it she'd been hoisted over the wall, and they were back out on the street.

Okay? Rhonda urged anxiously, gripping the nape of her neck to turn her face up. Fucking bastard! Rhonda repeated, looking her in the eye. I'll beat the fuck out of him.

She reflected that, the very next morning, before they woke her up to help them with the paper route, Rhonda would have told Becca what happened, and Becca would privately gloat. Rhonda would feel genuine distress. Becca would gloat. The funny thing was she felt superior to both of them. They didn't know anything really.

She did the hill part of the route, as usual. The sprinklers splattered into life, a dog barked, a man opened a door and shouted back at someone to make some eggs and toast.

VANILLA TOFUTTI

Stuart Fritsch perceives the ordinary. He has a lot of hair, which is not to be expected. He does not wear glasses, either. He does not shave and has not for three years. He is attracted to Jennifer Purvis because she has long blonde hair, small breasts and composes herself in primary colors.

Shall we go to a movie? says Jennifer.

Yes, says Stuart.

Stuart can see movies only if he is masticating, and it is not unusual for him to finish three packs, or thirty sticks, whichever comes first, of Carefree sugarless cinnamon-flavored gum. Jennifer, on the other hand, prefers sipping a Diet Pepsi because she often leaves her mouth open, which is commonly found to have a drying effect. She is not conscious of her reasons for drinking Diet Pepsi, however, and prefers to think herself a model of female virtue. If Jennifer admires the male metabolism, then Stuart admires the female position.

I am envious of Stuart Fritsch and Jennifer Purvis. I am envious of complementary relationships, and I think that I will sit between them at the next movie.

Stuart Fritsch sends his dog into the water.

Jennifer Purvis wonders if the water is cold.

Stuart Fritsch opens the bottle of Andre.

Jennifer Purvis wonders if she remembered some Kleenex. Outhouses are not at all apparent.

Stuart Fritsch notices the beginnings of lines around Jennifer Purvis' eyes, and he extends them. He thinks it amazing that, if he extends the traces of Jennifer's squints (her contact lenses react badly to the sun), she resembles his mother. This is a sign.

It is lucky Stuart Fritsch only perceives the ordinary, for otherwise he would be bored. I am obsessed by the ordinary because it is inherently boring. I define boredom by pursuing the boring; this I consider intelligent. But I would like to know which of the two, Jennifer or Stuart, is more boring. On the other hand, if one is interested in boredom, can one truly understand it?

Red roses. Red lips. Stones. Coffee. Horses. Water-proof watches. Dogs. Paper-clips.

How many times do these images cross their minds? This is the key. During her period, Jennifer thinks often of stones, equally often of the cream in her coffee. Stuart, depending on the tie he wears, visualizes roses when extravagant, paper-clips when practical. Stuart, not prone to biological vicissitudes, also thinks of a green Toyota truck and his mother, who always wears Estee Lauder, the perfume he has given Jennifer but which she herself never wears because it makes her sneeze. Jennifer dreams of a yellow MG Midget. She wears no perfume because she believes in the power of natural odors. If Stuart's imagination were of a higher order, he could project Estee Lauder on to Jennifer. As it stands, he leaves me to do this. Jennifer sneezes.

The car relationship speaks for itself, need not be analyzed. I am intrigued by Stuart's liking of paper-clips, a) in terms of their functional properties and, b) because this image is perhaps related to marriage, i.e., the joining of two or more flat surfaces upon which are typewritten characters. Normally one joins typewritten pages together so that they do not face one another. The depth of the typed words depends upon the weight of the bond used. Jennifer's visions of stone(s) are, likewise, unconscious materializations of self-identity. I might add, however, that this self-identity is actually based upon the one's conception of the other's identity. Jennifer looks at Stuart and sees a stone. Stuart looks at Jennifer and sees her paper-clipped.

A solution to the question of who is the most boring, then, lies in the comparison of the actual images themselves, rather than of the conceivers (namely, Stuart and Jennifer) themselves.

I find myself in a yellow MG Midget racing along a mountain road, then in a green Toyota with my dog barking in back. I look at red roses and send twelve to my mother. I let my natural odors accumulate. I do not take cream in my coffee, in this way understanding its significance. I'm equally bored by all these actions, at the same time recognize the inconsistency of my method. I conclude it is difficult to understand the true nature of boredom if one is consistently bored, even if for inconsistent reasons. It is in my interest to be interested, as this is what I am predisposed towards being in being bored. And yet, if boredom is complementary, then, in fact, I am interested by nature and must, naturally, continue to live in boredom which will make any objective understanding of boredom impossible.

Stuart Fritsch buys waterproof watches although he does not swim, and forces of habit still require his taking off his watch before entering the tub. Jennifer Purvis has two pairs of sunglasses: one with pink frames, which does not filter sun; the other with mirror-lenses, which make clouds look light blue. However, if

Jennifer looks at Stuart's bathwater with her mirror-lenses she will see it grey, because Stuart's bathroom has only a single 60-watt bulb. If Stuart's watch is not inundated, Stuart will never know if the one year warranty has validity. These two elements — light, water — are essential to the understanding of boredom. Thus we also comprehend the importance of water-proof mascara (which Jennifer does not admit to wearing) and, to a lesser extent, a bald head and a hat, neither of which Stuart owns. There are always such disturbing anomalies in my schema, and I am interrupted, in any case, by a picnic.

The picnic, an activity arranged by Jennifer last Sunday, is currently in progress and has been for the past half hour. In fact, I made an announcement earlier on (see "Stuart Fritsch sends his dog into the water. . .") and the reader is encouraged to refresh his memory of this occasion, as it is vital to the understanding of the following.

The unfortunate flaw in the water-proof watch is that I can't hear it tick. (11:40 a.m.)

s'il vous plait beaucoup vouloir alouette l'amour la vie la guerre alouette (ll:51 a.m. Alouette may refer to a garlic-spiced cream cheese or to a play about Joan of Arc by Anouilh, in which case Jennifer has forgotten the L'.)

Should I kiss your wrist? You need a watch. Waterproof? Swiss? (11:52 a.m. Stuart's thought of "Swiss" may refer to Emmeutaler or to Gruyere or to an actual Swiss time-piece but I cannot see into their picnic basket to discern if these are actual possibilities and I had thought they had only brought apples.)

I begin to see merit in paper-clips, and am motivated to change my method.

We are going on a picnic, to a pasture at the foot of the hills, sodden green, stubbled with dandelions, with a few horses watching us from the other end, where they stand by an old chicken-wire gate. The brown one comes towards us, now, and we shall give him our apples and be content with the champagne you brought and now are trying to open.

Looking in the mirror we remember your eyes. Is this the only way, now? To play Brahms Piano Concerto Number Two and remember a horse in a field and look into our own eyes, my, your own eyes and me see you, you me, because there is no difference. It is too simple: we are against ourselves. If I were an eyeball, a single blue eyeball, I should likewise be afraid. Once I stood at the back door which was glass and stared through it into the broken garage door window and I saw an eye. A single eye, cold, oblivious, suspended in the dark black hole of the broken window. Every morning I would do this — stare, for five or ten minutes, smile, plead, cry. Nothing was gained. No insights were achieved. Now, as I stare in the mirror, I believe, truly, that these are your eyes, even as they are everyone else's.

This is why we are afraid at the picnic. Even the horse slows down as he comes nearer, begins cropping the grass, looks up occasionally and pricks his ears at our voices. I can see his breath because it is a cool, damp morning in April. It is very simple to be the horse and I hear my voice which is so low and hesitant it is a background noise, the chewing of the horse. It does not catch the listener's attention, but hangs in the air like the thick, heavy moisture, neither rising nor falling, suspended, attaching itself to the listener, becoming his atmosphere. When the champagne bottle pops the horse startles and backs up a few steps.

You take off your t-shirt and stretch out in the sun, warming your skin, which you would like a darker brown. You wear humorous t-shirts and you are only sincere when we are alone. But I do not care about sincerity. I have looked into the garage window too long and sincerity is expressionless, inexpressible, non-existent and it does not matter to me how you try to shape it, create it, because your attempt is only words on your t-shirt. You have no control. I have all. You feel the sun right now, you say, it is July, you say, and I laugh because you are wrong. It is morning, raining, April, there is a horse standing, not far away, chewing dandelions, blowing smoke, the trees are stark, black, skeletal because they have been struck by lightning and will no longer grow leaves, only red and purple flowers, maybe roses, maybe chrysanthemums, depending. I unfold my black umbrella and hold it above me, though it would be more useful to hold the umbrella straight out in front of me, with a stiff arm, because it is not raining down through the air, but horizontally. You are sketching me and this, my current position, is what I choose to see on your sketch pad. My impression, charcoal smudged, nebulous, blurred by the watery air, an impression we all see because I see it and you are here and obviously you see what I see because I see you.

The sun is hot enough and while the river rushes by we can see in your eyes that you understand. It does not matter, voice; only the eye. Your eyes, because they have penetrated mine and accepted what is behind them. I throw Zonker sticks and he crashes heavily into the water, again and again, and does not mind the wet, not when it is this hot. I can see you are afraid for my dog, but he swims well, and if you look into my eyes you will not be afraid. I have seen you looking into the black water from the bridge and we both understand drowning. Water is black only in the shade of trees, under a sky of clouds. Today is blue, is hot, a shadeless hour, your eyes are equally blue, shadeless at this moment. Yet infinitely expressive; I can see my multifarious thoughts all mirrored in your eyes and I know we are one. One cannot exist alone, one does not exist alone, and I know myself only in your eyes, by this knowing you. The mosquitoes here are vicious. I slap them away. I admire you, who are impervious to their bites, whose curves are so clearly delineated by this sun. I wonder if I should throw my watch in the water for Zonker. If it is waterproof, yet perhaps it will not resist bites. The champagne is getting warmer, we must drink fast. The apples are no good, too bad; soft, spongy apples, fruit for the earth. I throw an apple into the pond and it sinks immediately. Zonker is not fast enough; he splashes in the water with a stupid expression, surveying the spot on its impassive surface where he believes the apple to have hit. The stupid expression, an innocence I find amusing. I lie down, absorbing the sun, watching you watch the pond, and we are one.

Last night I dreamed of being paper-clipped to a sheet of EZ-erase. And then I was making love to you, first face to face, then curled up, my stomach against your back. I think the latter position is better, because otherwise you are too close to see, or perhaps I see you too closely. But, Jennifer Purvis, why do I dream of you?

Stone ghosts. The moonlight has impaled the eyes of the horse, which reflect back upon us with a hard, brilliant innocence. Night horse. The stones have grown, tighten about us, large amorphic women, bulbous earth women, slim, pale, tubercular girls, they grow tall, tall, using up their roots, and come toward us, the expressions in their folded, chipped, striated faces suspended in ultimate extension, eternally set. I see your pale face and wonder, Stuart Fritsch, why?

Boredom depends on the color of one's eyebrows. If Stuart has black eyebrows, as he does, everything he says and does will be intensified, will seem excited. Blond eyebrows like Jennifer's, on the other hand, require that meaning be attributed to the reflection of light in the eye. Blond-eyebrowed people do not communicate well when in the dark, whereas dark eyebrowed individuals, if also having pale faces, will attain mysterious depths, like typed words on white sheets of paper, whether illuminated by a 60-watt bulb, a 150-watt bulb, a single candle, or by street-light coming through a crack in the blinds. If we define, as I do now, boredom as the lack of the individual's ability to perceive variations of intensity in the expressed or non-expressed feelings of a fellow human being, then Stuart is more bored than Jennifer. Jennifer, however, having blond eyebrows and not wearing any perfume, should excite Stuart's interest. If, in other words, Jennifer is boring, Stuart must be interested in Jennifer to find her so. While Jennifer, who perceives many variations in what Stuart expresses, not only in his eyebrows but in his t-shirts, must, essentially, be bored.

The next time I go out with Jennifer and Stuart it is for Haagen-Dazs ice cream.
I would like chocolate.
I think I'll try the Tofutti. Vanilla.
Single cones?
Yes. Yes.
No. I would have preferred Coffee with Hazelnut, but my

business is only to observe, not dictate. Jennifer resisted at first. She thinks it a bit cold to eat ice cream. The weather is more conducive to going for a walk in the cemetery. Jennifer would search for her identity in the stones. Stuart would make rubbings and paper-clip them together. As it is, however, we must deal with what is at hand: the ice cream. Which taste is more boring, chocolate or vanilla tofutti? This is not altogether a fair question, as tofutti is not made from milk, therefore cannot be classed as a "taste" among tastes of ice cream. If I compare tastes, I shall be accused of inconsistency/subjectivity. If I analyze the relationship between the taster and the taste, I shall be accused of the intentional fallacy. I suggest that your approaches to naming my methods be paper-clipped. I am only interested in boredom, and I am either interesting you with this boredom, or boring you with this interest. It is only a matter of taste.

Say I am vanilla tofutti, and you are Jennifer Purvis. I am created to be tongued by Jennifer Purvises, and I am now fulfilling my destiny. I feel myself, at first, in a gentle process of diminishment, then realize, soon, that I am expanding, mixing with salivic juices, Diet Pepsi and stomach acids. As she sucks the rest of my pure vanilla tofutti self out from the bottom of her cone, I at once complete evacuation of this place and inhabit completely her stomach space, wherefrom a new process of evacuation, and further expansion, is begun. So, Jennifer, how do you like me?

Say you are chocolate ice cream and I am Stuart Fritsch. I wonder if I feel the cold of this substance, or am I feeling the heat of my tongue? As I lick this, as more and more passes through my mouth, is my mouth cooler or the ice cream warmer? Does ice cream change color in my stomach? Chocolate ice cream is brown. Everything that comes out is brown. But the browns are not similar, and the latter brown is the true brown. As this ice cream loses its individual shade of brown, in amassing itself with other eaten things it also loses its individual taste, and becomes universal. Unless digestive systems are individual in their universality. But I am not prepared to prove this one way or the other. Even if I made the attempt, nothing would be proved, I conclude, because in the process of deciding to focus on original taste — taste going in — I realize this may also be universally individual. Chocolate is like a rich, dark soil that is mixed with sugar and milk. I am not going to go further than that.

Was it more boring to be chocolate ice cream or Jennifer? I, personally, found it more interesting to be vanilla tofutti. I had a clearer sense of identity. I was more bored being Stuart, because I was forced to be interested in defining the taste of chocolate ice cream, because once I attempted to define, I found it impossible: it is, or it is not, and even when it is not, it is. I would rather be in a cone, or in Jennifer's mouth, or in city sewers, indifferent to my identity because my identity is always in process, depends upon what capacity I fill; because I have no control over my identity I gain infinite identities, and each one of them is true, clear in the moment of their being. But I might be just as happy being Stuart or Jennifer, if Stuart is Jennifer and Jennifer is Stuart. The true nature of boredom is this: to be one and not the other. In purely objective terms, boredom cannot exist, because we define our existence in terms of other existences, and others define themselves in terms of our existences, and we all define or are defined by each others' existences. Always bored and interesting or interested and boring, but never both bored and boring or interested and interesting at the same time. Or.

I look into the eye, intensely interested, and it looks back at me, indifferent. Or I am vanilla tofutti, we are all vanilla tofutti.

Shall we go to a movie? Jennifer Purvis asks.

Yes, we should, Stuart Fritsch responds.

They choose a seat in the front row, center. Stuart Fritsch notices that Jennifer Purvis is wearing Estee Lauder and a sweater the color of a red-rose. He does not know Jennifer wears contact lenses, but he does extend the lines around her eyes, lines created by the interaction of her contact lenses and the grey light of the film, an old black and white Renoir about a picnic in a cemetery. Stuart chews his gum. Jennifer sips her Diet Pepsi. Stuart was not actually looking at Jennifer when he extended her lines, but at the etiolated woman on the screen, who may also very well be wearing contact lenses which are responding to cloudy ultraviolet rays. Anyway, Stuart sees his mother. Jennifer, of the blond eyebrows, which signify nothing, has gained an expression by wearing contact lenses. How long has she worn contact lenses? Could this have something to do with her not being able to perceive expression in the eyeball in the broken garage window? At that point she did not wear contact lenses, but she did look through the glass of the back door. Perhaps this is why she also perceives people as animate stones, or stones as animate people. Jennifer is a hidden person, she conceals the fact that she must look through a glass. She believes she is in control. Actually the eye in the broken garage window is in control, because Stuart controls it and she can't. Ha ha.

Paper-clip me, I am pleading to be paper-clipped: I must know, I must know if I am bored or boring, I must know if I face the second sheet or if I lie against it, my back to its face. I must know my position.

I go in and sit down between Jennifer Purvis and Stuart Fritsch. Jennifer offers me a sip of her Diet Pepsi, and Stuart proffers a stick of chewing gum. I hesitate a moment, and then I make the necessary choice.

WANDA & HER IMAGINATION

Wanda was a little girl who lived with her parents in a sunny house beside seas of rustling corn. Wanda liked to read stories and play in the fields with her dog, Corky, catching bugs and crickets and mice. One day when Wanda had just caught a grasshopper another little girl came up behind her and said "boo," making Wanda jump and allowing the grasshopper to escape from her hands. Wanda had never seen the girl before. She was wearing a short yellow sundress and carrying a black umbrella to shade herself from the glare and had appeared as if by magic in the middle of the field and said "boo." "Who are you?" Wanda asked. "Nobody," she said. "Who are you?" she asked. "Nobody," Wanda said back. "You talk funny," the little girl said and started to giggle and poke at her with the umbrella. "So do you. Stop that," Wanda said. "I will," said the little girl, and she did. Then the little girl said, "You talk funny and I don't want to play with you because I bet it's catching," and with that she skipped away, swinging her black umbrella behind her.

Wanda watched the little girl until she disappeared and she never saw her again.

Once, years before, Wanda's voice had been recorded on tape. To tell it straight, Wanda had been five years old and had said "I don't know" to every question her mother had asked her in the hope of preserving her child's voice for posterity. Later the tape became a family joke and even when Wanda was much older her parents played it to entertain company, just like most parents present slides or Super 8 films of their children to guests and then observe how cute the kids were and how it was a pity they grew up. On such occasions Wanda would run out of the room because she hated that childish voice and it mattered not a jot that she was now ten years old because in her heart she knew she still sounded exactly the same.

So it was that the strange little girl's pronouncement had only confirmed Wanda's worst suspicions about herself, and when she came home from playing that day she decided to plug her ears with cotton because she never wanted to hear her own voice again. But the cotton only trapped her voice inside her ears, where it buzzed unpleasantly, and Wanda decided to speak as little as possible.

In the meantime Wanda discovered she had muffled her mother's, her father's and their friends' voices as well — friends whom she had never liked anyway because when they came over they sat down and played pinochle with her parents, who told her to go work on jigsaw puzzles depicting things like seasides and kittens and maps of each of the fifty states. But no one noticed that Wanda couldn't hear them since she nodded and smiled obediently when she saw their mouths opening and shutting at her. For Wanda it was just like watching television with the sound off: things seemed strangely toy-like, or as if in the world of dream.

Wanda did this for a whole week. By the end of the week she had learned to lip-read and although having decided never to listen to her parents again, she realized she could still understand them, and so amused herself instead by pretending her mother spoke with her father's voice and vice versa. Yet since Wanda couldn't hear when her parents came up behind her and since she couldn't follow what they said when they turned their backs she became as nervous and jumpy as a starling, and since she couldn't sleep at night for imagining what she wasn't hearing she reread all of her Nancy Drews and bruise-colored crescents formed under her eyes, making her look malnourished. That was not too far from the truth, either, since chewing and swallowing food bothered Wanda as much as speaking did and she ate very little. Of course, Wanda's mother noticed she ate more like a bird than a little girl, but she only figured out what was really up when she was feeling Wanda's forehead for a temperature and spotted the cotton plugs in her ears. She removed them instantly, even though Wanda begged her to leave them because she hated getting bathwater in her ears.

No, the cotton was out for good and all.

Now Wanda only felt her voice in her throat and it wouldn't have seemed so bad anymore except that all the other sounds swooped down on her eardrums with the heavy beat of wings and hungry, beady-eyes of vultures. Or you might compare it to climbing up the beanstalk and finding yourself in a world of giants where sounds are proportionately louder, where every sensation is heightened ten-fold.

To stave off this horrible effect, Wanda began to speak again.

For instance, while her mother pan-fried onions Wanda told her the plots of every cartoon she could remember; yet when Wanda paused for a second worth's breath the sizzling of the onions in oil instantly cast her into a pit full of rattlesnakes. While her mother straightened the living room Wanda could list the names of rocks she had collected and identified in her mineral guide for all she was worth, but here even when she paused for a

half-second worth's breath the vacuum roared like a rogue ele-
phant on a rampage which, as she well knew from her books,
could crush a man as easily as a can of soda-pop. And if left alone
in her own room, Wanda had to talk or hum to block out the
chirping of birds and crickets and the wailing of dogs and cats
beyond her window — sounds that at any given moment might
choose to blow up into huge, frightening circus balloons and be set
alive by some evil sorcerer if she so much as stopped to swallow.

At first her parents delighted in Wanda's verbal turn; they
had begun to suspect an introverted, painful adolescence, indeed,
life-long psychological problems and summer allergies. Soon they
realized Wanda's rapid, often stuttering speech boded far worse;
her eyes feverishly glistened as she spoke and she constantly
looked over her shoulder as if someone else were listening. Her
parents could not stop her from talking even with time-honored
punishments such as sending her to her room, withholding
dessert, or forbidding television. But when Wanda was talking to
herself in the mirror one day, it struck her with a flash that her
mouth looked like a cat she had seen run over by a car.

The car had thrown the cat to the side of the street where
Wanda was playing jacks and it had lain there twitching, its mouth
opening and shutting with predatory spasms, as if it were still
alive, stalking a bird. And when Wanda's imagination leapt to the
parallel between the movements of Wanda's own jaw and the cat's,
it suddenly realized a whole range of powers never previously
considered: it could hatch life-threatening images not just from
what it heard, but from what it saw — indeed, every one of
Wanda's five senses was a fertile egg ready to crack!

So the next day when the sweet, spicy odor of her mother's
pie in the oven flooded the house, it made Wanda think of Gretel

baking in the witch's oven while Hansel, unable to save her, watched helplessly from behind the bars of his cage. When a piece of the pie was actually put before her and she was told to eat it, it made Wanda feel that the slices of apple between her teeth were tender bits of Gretel's flesh and nothing but. Where Wanda had once been wont to go to bed overexcited and chattering well into the morning hours until her talking had exhausted her, or the tape of children's carnival tunes her mother had given her to play on her am/fm radio-cassette alarm clock had swirled and spun her to sleep, now bugs and lopped-off hands kept Wanda awake, crawling over her legs beneath the bedcovers, and although at every tickle or pinch Wanda sat up, turned on her light and threw off her sheets, she was always just a moment too late to see the cockroach or the hairy-fingered thing before it disappeared into the wainscotting or the corner shadow, and finally would sink cold and forlorn back into her pillow, leaving her light on and her blanket off so that at least nothing could hide. Calling her mother did no good because her mother only thought Wanda was talking to herself; as for getting out of bed and going to her mother herself — impossible! Wanda's imagination made sure of that, setting before her not only the perilous regions of the floor, but lining the hall to her mother's room with a row of ravenous doors.

So Wanda remained where she was, staring helplessly at a crack in the ceiling, until she could have sworn she saw the little girl she had met in the field hop over it with one foot and wink, which, on top of everything else, convinced Wanda that from A to izzard words were spiteful sneaks just waiting to tell on you. No indeed, her imagination nodded to itself with satisfaction, this time Wanda would not speak again. Or, if she must — there were a few necessary monosyllables — she would bend them like gumbies, in such torturous ways that all within hearing would wince uncontrollably. You can picture how Wanda's imagination sprang into the air and turned a double somersault at that! And here we might have left Wanda, except as it happened her parents tore their hair in despair and her fifth-grade teacher sent her to a part speech-therapist, part psychologist whose name was Ellen.

"Again, again . . . again," Ellen said to Wanda several times every afternoon. Wanda would stare at Ellen's lips and mimick their movements expertly, but would not, of course, repeat the sounds aloud without garbling them. At first Ellen tried prompting Wanda into pronouncing her words properly by reaching into a round earthenware jar that stood on a shelf beneath a chart which illustrated the correspondence of mouth movements to vowel sounds and producing an M&M which she then pinched between her forefinger and thumb and waved in front of Wanda much like a magician waves a coin before making it disappear and then reappear in the ear of an astonished child. However, Wanda was too old to be bribed with chocolate, so at last Ellen ate the M&M's herself — because after all they met at the end of the school day, by which hour she was usually hungry — and moved on to other tricks in her repertoire, playing those kinds of games that court the impulse to speak, or deliberately mispronouncing words and misnaming colors of M&M's so that Wanda might correct her involuntarily. Wanda did cough occasionally, but that was all, and even that was partly because Ellen chain-smoked, a practice not yet banned in public institutions as it is today.

On the other hand, Wanda's imagination was fascinated by Ellen's smoke, the way it made small circles that diffused into invisibility, and it plotted for Wanda's own voice to come out in some soundless smoky shape, like a genie from a bottle, then

ascend into the heavens and startle birds and skydivers with
Christmas greetings or P.A. messages similar to Wanda's school
principal's. But before it could fully conceive this bit of mischief,
there was a rainy day and there was a black umbrella leaning
against the wall behind Ellen's desk and, as Ellen was saying,
"Again, again, again," and Wanda was watching the smoke rings,
she suddenly turned instead to listen to the water dripping hyp-
notically from the roof gutter on to the mud below. Pluk, pluk,
pluk it went — or even thump, thump, thump, like the wagging
tail of Corky against the kitchen linoleum at the sound of a can-
opener. Ellen, carefully observing this change in her pupil, blindy
reached down into the earthenware jar for an M&M and pulled
out her hand screaming. A big black beetle clung to her index finger. Horrified, she shook it off on to the floor and then, quicker
than you could have said jiminy cricket, Wanda jumped up, took
the umbrella and slammed it down, impaling the wriggling bug
with its pointed silver tip. Wanda laughed; Ellen was speechless
with surprise. "Again," Wanda shouted, "again, again," and each
time she said "again" she slammed the umbrella down until with
a sudden spasm it burst open just like a great big black hole in the
floor.

     No one could have blinked an eye faster than Wanda leaped
into that hole — and no one who ever knew Wanda ever heard of
her again.

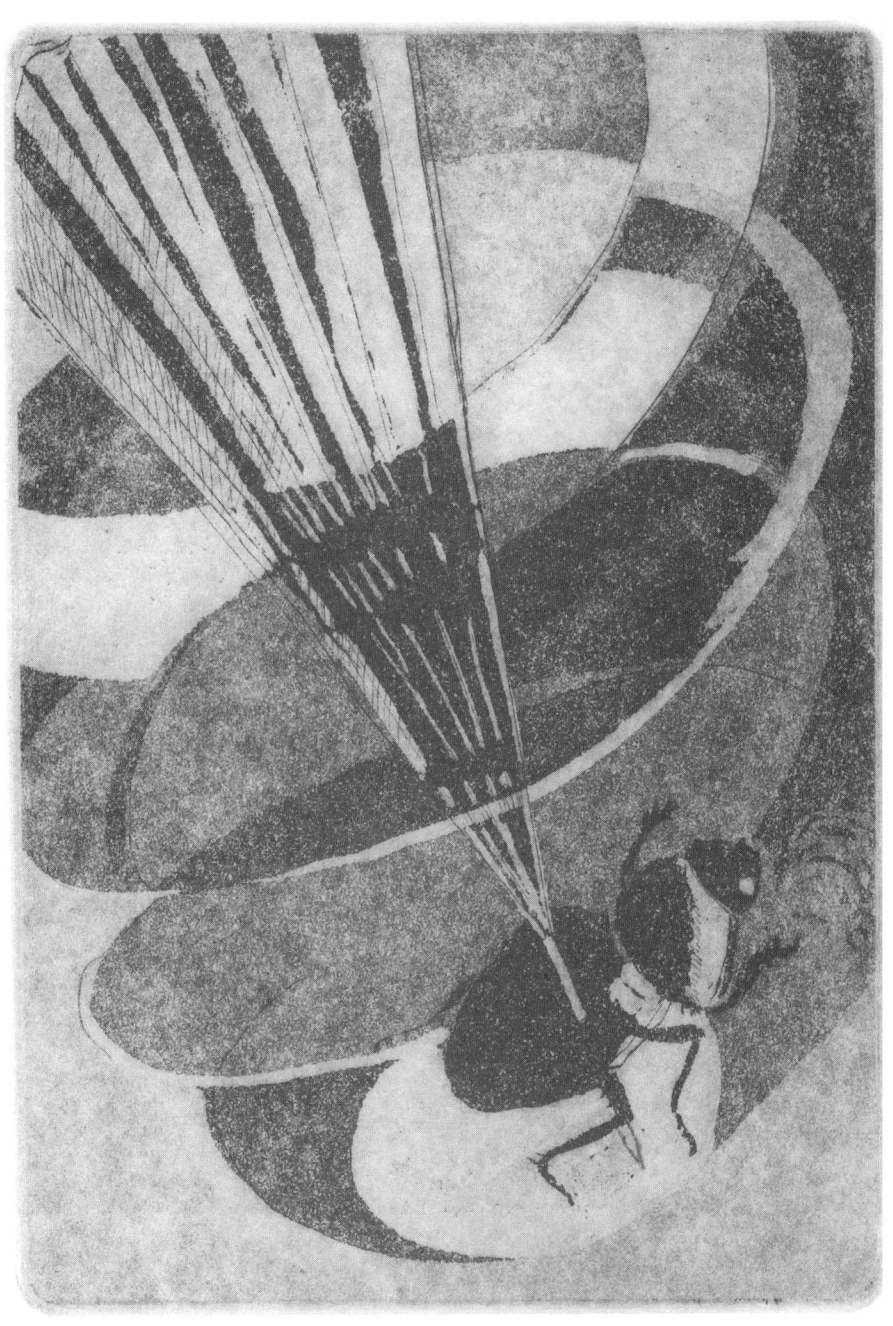

HOW GLORIA GROWS LONG NAILS

How does gloria grow long nails?
She doesn't really even know why she's growing her nails because none of her close friends has ever grown long nails, not even Diana, and early on her mother instilled in her the impression that long nails were unladylike, while her sister is in fact too physically active for them, so the only thing she can pinpoint with any certainty is an initial image of her fingers splayed out upon the little cherrywood desk next to the kitchen where she sits training an ear on the cooking and then suddenly seeing her nails grow, watching them slowly unfurl like seedlings in time-lapse film or stretch out the way shadows do when one moves back, a groping continually extending multi-legged predicate of an abstract subject which at this moment she can only identify as herself, unless it's her husband, whose treatment of the elderly household cat, the short-lived pats, the laconic strokes he bestows pragmatically upon its back despite the poor thing's being an indoor pet, declawed when they had still lived in the apartment, should have made her question his character even then, or unless it's the trauma of the cat's declawing itself come back to haunt her, since after she had willingly agreed with him to do it, for months, indeed years the cat's mistrustful, panzer-green gaze had followed her so that even now she mitigates with extra tins of catfood and who's to say she's not compensating in other ways, too, although admittedly during these summer afternoons of writing when she's interrupted by her

son's pinging of rubberbands at the very cat in question she finds herself still unable, still too exhausted to get up and save it, knowing that the energy it would take to shout at her son might easily stop the nails from growing, reaching further with every word as relentlessly as seedlings push through hardened mud towards the sun, so that only when she inadvertently looks up at the slammed door and out the window to see her son criss-crossing the brown-stalked field outside, thrashing an umbrella in the dry weeds and flushing out moths in panicked flurries, batch after batch of frantic souls fluttering before the whims of her own man-child, does she feel the energy that seeps from her body and into her nails cease, giving way to a light-headed exhaustion, the sensation of having been bled for hours by some malevolent creature from a Victorian novel

      she breaks the first peeling the plastic cover off a can,

      and then she splits the second on a hot frying pan

might begin again with a statement of the type found in women's magazines about women grown hostile, or simply unused to taking account of their bodies, and the project of restoring femininity to their various parts being difficult, and indeed who can blame her if her own first step towards aiding these growths so seemingly begun of themselves, when to fortify her resolution over the perilous weeks which immediately follow the incipient visions of women, in this case a vision of her nails growing like the tales of Scheherazade in spite or perhaps because of the executioner's threat, she turned to a fashion magazine, BAZAAR, the covergirl's smile having seemed strangely familiar, having beckoned to her from the supermarket kiosks as if to confide some secret while the letters above her face flashed out, winking like charms on a dancer's bracelet until held in her hand they became just another word, fell still as a trapped animal, pulsing and angular yellow A's a trio of paralyzed, uncomprehending eyes hunched between the chiseled bars of a B, Z and R that claimed the first, last and middle positions of a fashion sense which promises NO FAIL NAILS! if she apprentices herself to the magic spells and arcane properties of the milk and tuna one normally reserves for children and house-ridden cats, if she withstands her nails'perverse will to chip and peel off into small crepuscular segments, and if she conquers her own virulent urge to bite or cut them down to the slightest sliver of white, an impulse strong enough to have forced her to remove the scissors from the too accessible desk drawer and put them in the darkest reaches of the kitchen pantry amid the innocent jars of her mother's home-made apple jelly where they lurk crocodilean, ever-ready to assist a return to the familiar and easily-expendable condition of nails that are simply signs of a healthy, functioning body rather than the pernicious growths she suspects them of being now, agents implicit with some subversive power that has seized her as host, if not accessary, a role markedly different to the kind she realizes she has typically played in life, where more like Diana's evening purse, or her pendulous earrings, she has been an accessory, always swinging from an arm or dangling from an ear of experiences other than her own, indeed quite detachable from herself and easily flung away by others, always gauging her fail-ure in their eyes before feeling it herself, never acknowledging to herself that beneath that great, ever-expanding vowel she hears as her heart there is a profounder resonance pushing against the man-made boundaries of its measure, push-pushing like the head of the cat against her leg

she's brushing her hair when the third nail gets caught, and three snaps in two as she pulls it out of the knot never suspecting in her life that the man she had married would betray her with her best friend, that the man who observes, "I'm glad you're taking an interest in something, Gloria," as he stands over her desk while she writes has always really meant he's glad to see her when she's losing weight, looking controlled again, kept-up like Diana, sophisticated enough for him to escort her to parties and experience those flushes of jealousy so beneficial to his circulatory system and akin to the pleasure he enjoys after she brings BAZAAR home and leaves it in the bathroom where its pages speak to him with other lips and breasts, lend his eyes that slumberous opacity she can still remember loving long before among evening shadows in a large, high-ceilinged room that had only a mattress and blankets and pillows and the last light making skin soft as butter and eyelashes brush against the cheek like whispers fluttering in a cinema until the end of the reel goes flick-a-flick-a-flick and the memories are over, stolen away perhaps for the best by her son's umbrella beating against the weeds strong and heavy with the cruel ritual of a medieval drum or a nursery rhyme and obliging her to align herself with its relentless rhythm, that soldier's rhythm, that rhythm of the defeated heart which, first mourning the early years of marriage, had then defensively filled her rooms with vases, paintings, books, antiques, the myriad of objects that formed the batallion of soldiers which sprang up about her like the virgin queen's guard and steadfastly forced his attention back into the indifferent meatloaf-and-potato-eating sideglance which ossifies the last remnants of intimacy into the skull-and-crossbones that once labelled poisonous substances or, in more ancient times, marked the banners of pirate ships under the name of Jolly Roger

the fourth cracks on the bread-board as she's chopping shallots for the broth,

the fifth snags in the darning yarn for moth-holes in the
socks

when all along she thought Diana was a glorious angel, a light too
brilliant to look at straight, resplendent with a kind of beauty that
enfolded all beholding within a slow warmth, a feeling that kissed
long and wet with goodness, innocence and true, pure joy, quivering joy ecstatic as the green of new spring leaves, erasing all sense
of bitterness or otherness at having been set apart from the natural
world and performing an alchemy that lay her out like some sleek
animal on the floor, basking in the young strong sun and attaining
a temperature so equal to her environment she expands out and
further out in a pool of warm liquid until the sense of distinct
being is lost entirely, soaks down into the pores of the wood and
transforms into a single pulsing energy, an entity alive through
and through with a strange but comforting purring vibration and
so given over to gravity that it's as if floating outside of that force,
at one with the angel herself, suspended in bliss with her name on
her lips, DIANA, and rolled round in earth's diurnal course,
DIANA, with the rocks and stones and trees, but alas Diana's
smile flutters at this and then separates from her face and flies off
like a little bat out the window and up into the round pale moon,
and as she hears the soft but quickening beat of wings the impulse
to leap up and catch Diana and destroy Diana takes the place of
her sublime union with the essence of life and she wants to tear
and rend instead, to torture with abandon, rip off its wings and
pierce the furry body through and through, and looking down at it
between her hands she sees them trembling on the cherrywood
desk, the nails just beginning to curl slightly, like lips beginning to
curl in menace or draw back in pleasure, and in the second before

Diana's image is banished by the smell of the baking bread rushing in from the kitchen she can almost swear her nails have absorbed that smile, and a pang of terror sends her eyes straight up and out through the steamed window panes to her son who swings the great black umbrella open and ponderously flapping over the stark field of frozen sticks and ice-cold stones like a large dead crow

she tosses the wash in the dryer and she shuts the lid too quick —

smack down it slams and there's an end to poor nail number six

despite of or because of Diana, she does not know, but they grow, go on lengthening, stretch through the seasons, twisted, grotesque in appearance, but strong, infrangible to opposing forces such as the obligatory applause which when she attends some theatrical performance with her husband she delivers by slapping her palms together like flippers, careful to bend her fingers back so that her nails won't tangle in that Iagoan smile of evil genius, that miraging, sycophantic smile of Diana's which having heard all her confidences hovers wordlessly over her husband's left shoulder, who himself squeezes his eyes shut to make love while she, ever-careful to ward off the threat, suspends her nails over his back like clusters of ripe fruit or pins them to her sides so that they become a grapevine clinging to its trellis or the martyr of her Catholic schooling, arms stretched taut on the cross fixing her body into an inanimate lower case "t" such as found in the skirts, pants, tops and tees which accouter BAZAAR's bare-boned sentences and where feeling no longer need exist as it no longer exists in the impervious glances of her husband whose taste for novelty betrays him even as his pupils leap saccadically from the food at his fork to her nails layed out against the dining room table like primitive flatware until he has finished eating and then she can't keep, although she tries, from asking him whether the trout was fresh enough, from rearing her fingers up on the tips of her nails, arching them like a hungry cat, although the nausea soon grips her intestines and mistrust of him squeezes python-like around her chest, tight, tighter, presses her to run from the room and only then will the bile recede for a time, later the same evening to rise back up when she is straightening a picture on the wall, the certainty that he will come in the middle of the night while she sleeps, wrestle her to the ground and brutally snip off her nails as he had had to do to the cat before it was declawed welling in her throat making her cough up a large clotted mass in the sink, its aftertaste so evil she knows it unnatural, but feels better, feels calm, licks her lips shut like an envelope and contemplates rational strategies for making nails invulnerable until her son skips in from the field to beg for the umbrella, takes it, holds it against the sunny sky like a parasol immediately after she says "yes" and there he is, an impressionist figure in a field of stiffened brush strokes which she can feel beneath the whorled skin of her fingertips like knots in wood dabbing at her heart, while in her mind the alphabet she taught him darts in and out like a snake's tongue, Z, Z, Z is for Zoo

        she puts paste on the silver and she rubs it shiny bright,

        but the seventh turns dry and thin, and then drops off for spite

because it is Diana, it is Diana she has to write about, to get out of her system how Diana's voice crept through the phone and rolled "tomorrow" off its tongue, how she wished it had been addressed to her but was denied as soon as Diana said with one gentle sweep, "isn't she taking Bobby to the zoo?" leaving her alone with the misery of being a third-person pronoun in which guise, for the time being at least, she knows she must wait as it is a job for patience and requires rolling up her pantyhose carefully, wearing cotton-lined rubber gloves when washing the dishes, at the last minute keeping inadvertent gestures from collisions with the clutter of her house, restraining from picking off price stickers and even from tasting sauces with her fingers yet — if one does break —swallowing the setback with pleasure, a bit of shell in which she just tastes the essence of the firm nut it shields, a core of will that will not be cracked open again, and in a moment, as she rests her hands on the desk and looks down, she sees that they are growing despite her anxiety, have become hard enough to tap gently on the cherrywood and for her to extract a fearless pleasure from the thin clicks of sound quite comparable to that she knows Diana took in telling about her lover, about her own husband, about how they sometimes met out in autumn's fields during harvest moons, full moons, witch's moons that turn flesh an unearthly shade and immobilize you in the surreal light of someone else's mind with wondering how he found it possible to make love to two in the same place under the same moon, yet no wonder because she is Diana, she is beauty, she is form enough to satisfy the imagination, she has the cool charm of a halcyon, immutable and nesting upon the dumbfounded glance, she is the very surface she rests upon, she hushes all stirrings of reason and looses all human bonds, dares time and gravity to disturb her expression and her limbs when she walks and when she laughs throws the sound easily out her throat to pass smoothly through the elements without registering so much as a scratch of roughness, crudity, or sincerity, yet for all that the brazen sound of a mistress, the expected rather than

99

desired laugh, a kind of vowel, indeed, but not the vowel, it cannot be the vowel keeping secret in her heart

eight gets ironed under the collar she's trying to press,

and nine rips in the zipper of her very best black dress
if only for the sake of her son she will resist Diana, she will refuse to paint her nails, not pink, purple, red or black, proving to everyone her nails aren't false nor in need of artificial reinforcement, as if their misshapen lengths don't already horrify everyone into stepping back when they meet her and then hurriedly forward in the wake of etiquette's skirts, a primitive fear she almost wheedles, is almost pleased to tease, all-but-cold embers she delights in fanning hot with gestures at once theatrical and civilized, an enviable choreography of hands, a tribute to the art of not telling to tell, her coyly lowered lashes, her fingernails spread proud as a peacock's tail but vengeful as pearl daggers hidden in folds of flesh, ensigns of possibility or evil omen, borders to be crossed and crossings which she glimpses in the eyes of certain men at her husband's parties who have parlayed love far enough beyond sentiment to win the pure and ominous form that scintillates like cut diamonds from such faces and from the glittering unintelligible eyes of such men, Diana's men, ever mute, lean and crouching in the corners of rooms like hyenas beneath Babylonian stars, women-men knowing how to bite the palest sections of thigh and arm with a torturer's delicacy, who can place lips on the palms of hands with the coolness of precious stones, whose tongues flicker warm, moist on the skin but for an instant before, with the clap and hiss of cymbals she dances away like a pagan goddess in her black silk dress, the huntress herself, a sleek panther swishing through jungle ferns and grasses, weaving and winding through the guests, stopping here, then there to crook her little finger at them with its long

hooking nail, enthrall all before finally, gracefully, whirling out of
reach and back into the arms of her husband, who holds her still,
whose blond and innocent hair, wheat-colored and woodgrained,
conquers her eyes for a breath long enough to look out the window through which honeysuckled air rushes, whirring the pages
before her with a frantic winging, and to her son making furrows
in the muddy earth with the silver point of the old umbrella, a
scene fading fast, fading like a photo exposed to days of sun until
she's entirely back sucking in flat tonic and hearing the suggestion
to go home, finds herself between sheets, her nipples aroused by
fingertips while his real attention fixes itself to the nails lying
across her belly because by the evening's end her having become a
woman possessed half-frightens and twice as much titillates him,
and Diana's strange sleepy smile and the state of anticipation she
means to provoke she continues to needle by slowly filing the curl-
ing nails into beautiful tines as he kneels at her side, by painting
them with the painstaking strokes reserved for the last great work,
brushing on crimson polish slowly and steadily and perfectly
while he awaits the consummate caress she has premeditated even
to the point of setting her nails flat on the white flesh of her stomach to dry hard, slick, sharp until, whetted long enough for any
appetite and worthy of executing acts of mythic proportion, she
readies herself for vengeance on mankind and looks up full into
his face entirely unprepared for the cat's rubbing up between
them, its shedding hair causing her to sneeze and break the spell,
making her realize she does not care for him to do this, it's not him
she cares for and suddenly the blood rushes back into her body
and her cheeks making her dizzy with clarity and shame
     and when the tenth nail is the only nail left to go,
     she bites it off herself so nothing stays to show

she must cut them off, be done with it, eschew all further responsi-
bility except, perhaps, the final ritual due such endings, to which
end she will entrust them to her son in a pin box, instruct him to
bury it in the fields while she sings the lovely vowels of "AVE
MARIA" from the window out at the August afternoon, at the
birds silenced and huddled on the power lines by the dark-knuck-
led thunderheads steadily approaching from the west, and then on
top of them to plant the umbrella so that it sticks up straight and
unyielding, blooms a great, uncompromising flower that indicates
her place amid the landscape of yellow weeds with a sign beautiful, static and sterile as the third A which distinguishes the word
BAZAAR, the law of her love yet in the sunny days ahead the
elongated shadow that will needle at her heart, her meek and
lonely heart, for it will not be done with and the easterly flow of
clouds continues on unmarked by such events, the setting sun
now strangely appearing to rise as the span of its aureole is
unveiled, its light brightening, expanding up, and they race
toward her faster and faster until, heralded by a blast of hail
against her windows, they threaten to roll over her like a massive
juggernaut, knocking down her heart to let in the name DIANA, to
let it out, pulsing like the unnameable source of her fingernails
that in off-pearl luster glow against the cherrywood, in pale twist-
ings like roots of forbidden plants push deeper underground,
press on past known goal, longer, stronger grow impossible the
breaking off even facing the bright days outside her son galloping
along dizzily at play breaking her heart indeed meek yet not meek
enough for still that word, needs a word she can't speak, can't
write, but a word needs to be to complete the work at hand to
mean no conclusion, means no stopping, no instrument long
enough no means to meet the needs of her nails made no sentence

103

exists doesn't meet a period existing yet must avoid further risk cannot scratch against the paper needs meanings me she needs to choose meaning unless the cat me waiting at her feet leaping pawing the pen from hand to floor to me it me is ME-OWW is large and open she is MEOOW jumping crouching pouncing setting the pen rolling again pounces and chews finishes and swallows licks and purrs purrs and kneads kneads and kneads

THE TALE OF HANS AND HIS
SISTER WILDROSE

I dream of her, her feet, her hands, her hair and her pale skin — but always in parts, and sometimes I recognize these hands, feet, hair and skin as mine and everything becomes confused. I dream in little broken bits, but then I dream that my brother is asleep in his room, and the hairy sailor is with me in mine and demands that I pull out my dresses, of which I have only three, and lay them on the bed. He bundles all three into a little wax bag and says, Follow me. But my brother, who will take care of him? I start to say but the room shakes and trembles with the pounding of hooves and then I hear the whinny of a horse and wake to discover that it is all the neighbor's doing, the furniture he is moving and the strange whistle which bursts from him like syrup from an overripe plum. The book, which I had been trying to read when I fell asleep, drops to the floor, its cover open, the quivering letters illuminated plainly in the moonlight.

Once upon a time there was a brother and a sister who loved each other very much. The brother's name was Hans and the sister's Wildrose, because her father pricked his finger when he plucked her mother a rose to mark the day of his daughter's birth.

Hans was much older than Wildrose, for all of her mother's children had died in-between. Hans loved his sister dearly and they played in the forest and made no other friends,

although the birds chattered and fluttered about them fearlessly and the deer grazed near the large rock where they sat. Here they amused themselves by listening to the rush of the river and watching for the leaps of the fish, and Wildrose told Hans all the secrets that the forest told her, but he bade her not tell her mother and father what she knew.

Wildrose loved her brother and obeyed him even though her mother and father were unhappy because the little girl, whose blue eyes laughed like the sea and whose long golden hair caught the sun and held it even in the deepest woods, closed like a stricken bud in the house of her parents. Yet how could her mother say to her father, "It is all your fault for pricking your finger on the vine the day of her birth," when he had pricked his finger and picked her the rose only in a gesture of love? Indeed, the consequences of this could not have been foretold.

Would you like some more coffee? Are you going to be getting home late tonight? After the third question he shakes his head and turns up the volume on the TV: *In Los Angeles, thousands have died in a catastrophe that seismologists failed to predict. Many of the earthquake's victims still lie buried in the rubble, and as the search for them continues, the extent of this tragedy cannot yet be told.*

I wanted to say to my brother, What if our parents were living there now? but I knew this would only make him angry. He does not like me to think of them. After he finishes his cereal he turns off the TV and leaves for work.

But when it came time for Hans to go out in the world and seek his fortune, Wildrose grew sickly and lost the color in her cheeks. "I must go with you," she told her brother, "or I shall die." Wildrose was yet a child and her parents were angry when Hans told them he was taking her with him to seek his fortune. His mother cried and his father said, "You are to blame for all our unhappiness. Take her if you will, but know you must never be separated, for now you can only belong to each other." His mother wiped her tears and made them each a little bundle of cheese and bread and gave Hans a jar of water to carry for them both, for Wildrose was too young to bear much weight. To Wildrose she gave the rose her husband had plucked on the day of her birth. "Keep to the paths," his father warned Hans, "and promise me that, no matter what happens, you will never leave your sister." Hans promised without a moment's hesitation and then they kissed their parents good-bye and set out to seek their fortune.

The morning flies by like a bird's shadow and then is gone, swallowed in the midday summer heat. I feel at a loss. Outside the sprinklers slash at the yellow lawns like whips, cold, wet, as steady as the rhythm it takes to sharpen knives, and I can't help but brush my hair to keep in time. When it stops though, the silence is enough to make me turn on the fan, climb into the sound as if into the jaws of a whale, I imagine, all warm and contained, if not safe, yet with the comforting gurgle of water around you, and the whale's ponderous heartbeat in your ears — you could live there quite nicely for a time. On television the Poles ride against German tanks and fighters on horseback. Then, cut to color, a thin old man with gaunt cheeks and hard eyes. *We were not frightened*, he says; *not even our horses were frightened*. That's when I began to dress and decide what to do with myself.

"Where shall we go?" little Wildrose asked Hans.

"To the sea-side," he said, "where the fish are plentiful and ships come from strange lands loaded with all that you could wish for."

"Dear Brother," said Wildrose, "I wish for nothing more than to live with you in peace and happiness. It is the forest that we know. Can we not stay here and live among the trees, where no one will disturb us, and we shall never want for firewood or food." For Wildrose was unhappy to leave the forest, even though she loved her brother.

"There is much you do not know," Hans replied. "Do not fear, little Wildrose, but let us stick to the path as Father told us, for it is only this way that we may find our fortune." So little Wildrose held back her tears and picked up a pine cone to take with her.

After putting on my sandals I go out into the hall to check the mail, but there's never any mail for us, only for them. There are three other apartments in our building. Just next door, for one, is a caterer. I first learned he was a caterer when he drove home in a white van with *Ernie's Catering* printed on it red. He's a strange man; through the walls I've heard him shout, *John! John!* as if he were calling someone into supper, which is curious because John is my own brother's name, but as far as I can tell no one else has ever gone in. Anyway, the caterer has a thin blond mustache and very fair skin; I've seen him protect it from the sun with an umbrella when he goes outside to load his van with plates, serving pans, silverware and such.

Then, upstairs, lives the burglar. Actually, I don't believe he's a burglar anymore, but he does move furniture all the time. I can hear heavy objects being scraped back and forth over the floors as he uncovers the hiding places for his loot. Now, though, I'm pretty sure he's a drug dealer and he's hiding drugs. He has long brown hair in a ponytail, and he wears big brown, thick-soled work boots. He has very soft eyes, a deer's eyes, and he stares at you, sitting on the stairs and smoking. What unnerves me is his high-pitched whistle — just like that it comes out, tuneless and sharp and sometimes mocking, like a bird call, or maybe a cartoon character's laugh, like the road-runner's, but I'm not certain because my brother never let me watch cartoons much.

So Hans and Wildrose journeyed toward the sea, but took a path which ran by the forest, and when they were hungry they found nuts and berries waiting to be picked and when they were thirsty, the water called out to them as they drew near.

After seven nights they came upon a fork in the road, where one path continued along the side of the forest and wound along a hidden route and the other led through a desert plain towards the horizon, where already Hans and Wildrose glimpsed the sea snapping in the morning sun.

Then there's the smell in the hall, a strong, sweet flower smell, maybe gardenia. I used to think another woman lived here, but there are only men's names on the mailboxes, and I suppose she just visits the drug dealer or the sailor who lives next door to him on the second floor. He's older, fat and hairy, walks with a limp — you can hear it on the stairs — but it is the tattoo on his arm that tells me he's a sailor, and when he brushed me once, going past me to get his letters, I saw the tattoo was a woman and for a moment I thought I could smell it, gardenia, and he winked at me as if he knew what I was sniffing at.

"Dear Brother," little Wildrose said, "should we not stay by the forest path a little while longer, so to be sure of food and water; for who can know how much further the sea lies, when there are no trees to tell the distance by? Perhaps we shall also meet someone on this path who will give us advice, for it is

plain no one comes toward us by the other."

"No little Wildrose, we must take the path which offers clearest direction. There the sea lies and surely in less than a day we shall be there, without having felt the lack of water or food. Should we risk angering Fortune by ignoring that which she sets before us?"

You can't think, he said. That is what he always told me. And it was because he was born when the war began and because I was born so much later, when my parents were already in America, old and past the hope of a future. And so he took me to the park and gave me gum and said you can't think because everything to be thought of has already shown itself.

I tried very hard to stop thinking ahead. I tried to look at things just the way they were, but it was difficult. Eventually my parents took me out of school because I didn't have friends and put me into a place where they played games with colored cards and numbers and alphabet letters. Still, I couldn't hide it from my brother. I told him, *I keep thinking about things, I can't help it.* So he gave me books to read and he said, *I will teach you how to stop. But never tell them*, he said, *she will cry*; and when he took me into his room he gave me pretty marbles with blue and green and yellow eyes in them, one after another, each for each kiss he gave me. Even so, when my mother saw us together she wept, although I swore to him I had told her nothing.

The books he gave me were so hard and dry I chewed and chewed on every pea and still I had to spit them out.

So Hans and Wildrose walked towards the sea by way of the desert and although they saw nothing but rocks and dry yellow grass, heard nothing but the hisses and rattles of hidden things, the sea remained steady before them and they were not

afraid. When the sun began to set the sea grew dim and finally disappeared into the darkness. That night there was no moon, and the darkness was complete. Hans and Wildrose stopped to sleep.

After my parents died, my brother forbade me to speak to him, except at night. Your voice belongs to the night, he said; you must only speak in the dark. So at night I spoke to him and he held me close to him in his bed and told me stories and said that we loved each other more than anyone else in the world could love.

We still don't speak in the mornings.

I hear someone come into the hall outside and there is a little rustle at our door. I wait, listening. After a few minutes I open the door and there is a little folded white waxed bag, the kind used for donuts. Drugs, I suspect; he's going to try and addict me, that's why he's been staring at me. Yet it turns out to contain a little plastic dish of olives and two pieces of baklava wrapped in a paper napkin. The caterer! I was always sure he was a kind man, though he is shy and never meets my eye. The olives taste nutty, slightly bitter, and I think to save some for my brother, but I don't; I don't even save the second piece of baklava. It's the first time I've done something like this, behind his back.

I start sorting through the box of stuff I've kept with me from childhood and I find the tarot cards but not the yellow book which tells me how to read them. I shuffle them anyway and lay four cards out, one for the past, one for the present, one for the future and one for me. Yet even as I lay them out I realize I have forgotten whether the future lies to the right or to the left of the present, or whether the present is the first card and the past and future follow. There are the pictures, but I can't remember their

meanings; my fortune is told but I can't tell it anymore. Oh well.
A nice warm feeling rises in me, up from the caterer's food, and I
might just as well take a nap.

**But in the early hours of the morning a hot dry wind
sprang up and blew violent gusts of sand against Hans and
Wildrose. By the time the sun rose the air was filled with dust
and they could not see but a few steps in any direction. "We
must wait," Hans told Wildrose, and he covered her with his
body so that the sand wouldn't sting her face. When the storm
had passed and the dust settled they looked toward the sea and
it seemed no nearer than it had the morning before. Hans
frowned and for a moment thought of going back. "No,"
Wildrose said because she loved her brother, "I can taste the salt
of the sea on my lips and we will be there soon, if you still wish
to go." They drank from the jar of water Hans carried and as
there was still water left, Hans became cheerful. "Indeed, we
shall be there soon," he said.**

But later things changed. At night when I went into his
room he often seemed angry with me, and in the morning his eyes
were hard against me. Of course, it was her all along. I don't
know exactly when it started with her, but now when I open the
door and that sweet smell comes out at me dull and spreading,
like a bruise, I can't deny it. There my brother lies so peaceful in
bed asleep, his long eyes closed into the cool, slanted lines of his
lids, a cat's eyes which at any moment might open and seize me in
the night. I know one day he will be my death, if only because of
her motionless shadow, lying in the same position I recognize
myself to have slept in. Our childhood is behind us and our parents are gone, too, and her shadow grows the longer the more I
close the door, but I know it will not happen until what? All I can

picture is the Poles riding their horses against tanks.

The garage sale has been held across the street for the last two days now, and so I suppose I'll have a look. The little girl is once again selling lemonade and her mother is reading a magazine, but I wait until another woman has arrived, before going over myself. I pick up one of the books in the pile. It is small, has thin pages, a green fabric cover; I see my hands, my hands on the book. I open it up and look at the signature, which is long with spidery thin letters and the year, 1939, but the book is unreadable, written in some foreign language. I think, maybe I will buy this book; it is only a dollar, and the pages feel smooth to my touch.

What do you think about that earthquake? I knew it was coming. I always told my husband there was no way I'd be fool enough to live in California, the little girl's mother says into the air, to either of us. I smile at her and nod, but with a shock I realize the other woman is the drug dealer, with his hair all down.

And what do you think about the Poles riding their horses against the tanks and fighter planes? My voice scratches to get out at first, in embarrassment, then gushes like over-poured coffee.

I can't say I know anything about that. She turns to the drug dealer who holds up a couple of pine cones. *Oh that, you can have those. My daughter brought them back from some trip to the mountains we made,* she gestures indifferently.

How much? he asks the little girl.

A quarter? she tips her head to the side, like a robin.

He whistles. *Deal,* he says, tossing her a coin.

Sure enough, already after one more night Hans, too, could taste the salty air and soon they heard the cries of gulls flashing through the air and swooping like silvery blades in battle. A moment later the sea lay before them, vast and glittering.

Many ships could be seen in the bay.

"Dear Brother, we have come to seek our fortune, yet what shall we do?" Little Wildrose asked, but her words came to her own ears in an unknown voice and she shuddered to hear it.

You can't think. You don't know how to be logical. You don't know how to think, he said when he used to take me to the park, leading me by the hand and giving me gum to chew. People looked at me and I don't know what they thought. *No,* that's not the right answer, he'd say if I tried to answer his questions. *If you don't know what to say then don't speak.*

Lemonade, the little girl calls after me.

Not today, I wave, starting back across the street with the book, but he beats me to the door of our building and opens it, bowing. *I know what you're talking about,* he says, *and I think it's a shame.*

"I shall become a fisherman," Hans said, "and we shall live in a cottage by the sea." And Hans sniffed at the air and laughed aloud, but her brother's yearning glance at the harbored ships tore all the sweetness from Wildrose's heart, and she clutched at the pine cone in her pocket, drawing comfort from its scratchy roughness against her skin.

In the hall the smell of the sweet perfume is heavy, almost falls like rain. I go into my bedroom, take off my clothes, lie down. I can still smell it in here, the sweet damp scent, holding me within its moist open mouth, covering my skin with a warm wet breath. But my fingers are cool, and I trace long cool lines down my body, like lines of mown grass. I can close my eyes and touch him this way, only just skimming his skin with my fingers, and wherever he is I can tell he feels them and turns toward me to touch my body in return, making the same long lines, and then, at

114

once, I feel nothing at all. And a thought comes to me, and I am not surprised to hear a knock at the door as if in answer. *Oh, but it's you.* My words chatter together like a couple of the marbles my brother gave me and repeat, click, click; click, click.

"Dear Brother, where is this cottage? And who shall help us find food?" Indeed, Hans and Wildrose knew no one in the city. The people rushed about them without noticing their worn clothes and tired steps and without stopping to offer them any words of advice, for while it was clear that they were strangers, strangers are common in cities near the sea.

"Don't ask such questions, little Wildrose," Hans said, "and do not cry, for Fortune only blesses those who have faith. Let us walk on among these people, for to be sure, someone will stop and ask us what we seek."

Hello, he says extending his hand, the nails encrusted with salt, the finger callused with the tying of many knots. *May I come in? I have something that will interest you.* He rolls out from behind him, with the tattooed arm, a vacuum cleaner. *I sell vacuum cleaners; may I sit down and tell you about them?*

I look toward the sofa, on which there is a stain I have forgotten to cover with the pillow. He would begin with something like this. I recall a voice saying that at the ends of wars sailors become salesman; but their tales, which yet they carry from door to door, still tell them.

The Yorick vacuum is different than any you've had before, he continues; *and it seems to me that you would be the kind of lady who would really appreciate the power and the cleanliness that the Yorick represents.*

I nod for him to go on.

What kind of vacuum, may I be so bold to inquire, do you use?

From Sears, I say, remembering the day my brother brought it home. *Ah,* he says, leaning back with the sound. *Then you will not realize how deeply, thickly the dust, the skin, the hair lie, nor know of the mites that feed upon them, invisible to the human eye.* When he pauses and I suddenly remember I have not brushed my hair yet and blush with embarrassment. *Indeed, the Yorick will vacuum up filth beyond mortal perception. May I demonstrate?*

And so the sister and brother continued through the streets of the city, and little Wildrose was fearful of the rough-skinned seamen and the smell of herring, the women who shouted at them from the street-market stalls, and the children who ran about with sticks and poked and pulled at her long golden hair so that she finally tucked it all beneath her coat. But at length a young man, who had passed them on the street previously, noticed Wildrose's frightened blue eyes and stopped to offer them help. "We are new to this city and seek work and a place to stay," Hans said hopefully. The young man gazed at them thoughtfully; then he said: "You may come and stay with my father and help care for him until you find your way, for he is growing old and would be glad of companionship after I return to my ship." The kind stranger took Wildrose's hand and bade them follow him.

No, I don't think —

Indeed, you owe it to yourself, my dear. He takes out a handkerchief and mops his face so I can see the woman on his arm.

Please, would you leave — I don't feel well. Maybe it's the caterer's food? Maybe the olives were poisoned, like they do to apples at Halloween, with a syringe? Maybe it is just a female problem.

Of course, I can always come back later, living here in the same building as we do. Then he takes up my hair. *Lovely hair! Let me teach you how to braid it.*

You must go, I say, I am dizzy, but as he pulls and combs out my hair with his fingers I begin to feel pleasure, the nausea subsides, and it does not seem so urgent that he go. He takes me to the mirror in my room. *This way, you see, and this,* he instructs me. *You see how simple it is!* Only after he has left do I regret not having asked him if he knows her, whether it is her perfume I smell in the hall, whether it is her image tattooed on his arm. One thing I do determine is to test the caterer's food on my brother. The dizziness it brings on is not so unpleasant, yet I want to know.

Would you like some more coffee? Something to eat? Weekends, we pretty much sit and watch TV. I've decided not to tell him about the salesman, and pick up the newspaper instead to look up my horoscope on the bottom of the page. *A stubborn refusal to listen to the truth sets you back. Hidden factors can spell danger. Read between the lines and follow your heart, no matter what the consequences.* Of course, horoscopes only work if you expect nothing, which is why only a voice that knows nothing can tell you what will happen. Only afterwards will you know what you've been told. Still, I snip it out with scissors and keep it.

The old sailor offered them his home with an open heart, for indeed his son was leaving on the next ship, and he welcomed their company and help. He said that Wildrose might cook for him and clean his house, while her brother went out with the fishing boats. The old man smiled at Wildrose and squeezed her hand in a rough, friendly grip.

Hans gratefully accepted the invitation and said to Wildrose, "You see how Fortune smiles upon us now, little Wildrose. Truly, we have nothing to fear."

I can't help picturing the drug dealer, how he is beautiful —
no, it can't be denied. I like how his helmet strap dangles beneath
his chin before he pushes off on his mountain bike. But I would
want him not to whistle, ever, because when he whistles he is
something else, like a wolf in sheep's clothing. Still, wolves, of
course, are only being true to their nature.

In the mirror I see moonlight gleaming on my hair; it needs
brushing, it needs braiding, it's all in a mess from my restless
sleeping. I wonder if he sleeps in the bedroom which would be
above mine.

Your strength is that you don't want anything, he used to
explain. *And there is nothing to know unless there is something you
want, and then that is all.* He's wrong though; I do want things.
And I know that he loves another woman and wishes me dead.
Being wished dead by your brother should be enough. It would
be enough if I could hate her, but I just hate myself. Her, she's just
a shadow, and he won't let me in close enough. This is why I figure he'll murder me, because he only lets me see her in parts.
Sometimes, though, I consider that maybe I only expect this death
because I want it, or perhaps I even want it to happen because it is
the only thing I can be sure will happen without having to want it.
In fact, I'm considering that it might be my brother, in cahoots
with the caterer, trying to poison me by way of those little wax
packages of food — especially since he himself has refused to
touch any of it so far. *Too fancy for me,* he says.

Poison can be subtle, I've heard, and it can be addictive. I
can't help it, I've noticed myself growing greedy for that rustle at
the door, for the pistachio-stuffed figs and the brie tartlets left
there. And if it is the drug dealer after all? The drug dealer's
clever and he's used to being wanted, I can tell; he may be fooling

me.

And so, for several years Wildrose and her brother lived contentedly and the old sailor entertained them with his many tales of the sea; yet Wildrose could never forget the forest and when the sailor fell to snoring, she'd beg her brother to tell her back again and again all the things she had told him when she was small. But Hans was restless and dreamed of other things. Often he gazed at the merchant ships preparing to depart from port, imagining only the day he would accompany them to the exotic lands of the East.

Wildrose knew this, for each day that Hans returned with his catch, he spoke less and strode about the old sailor's cottage with a heavier step. But she said nothing to him, for she could not bear the thought of his going away. Finally, it was the old sailor who asked Hans what distressed him and Hans said to him, "I want to join up with a merchant ship."

"Wildrose may stay with me," the old man reassured him, "you needn't worry. I shall take good care of her."

On the news they say that the animals knew the Earthquake was going to happen. In the Los Angeles Zoo the birds dashed themselves against the aviary enclosures, the big cats paced and snarled endlessly, the monkeys screeched hysterically between the trees, and elsewhere they say wolves ate their cubs and elephants tumbled and trampled their keepers. It all makes me feel so guilty, that I haven't given him a chance. I bring him the green book I bought at the garage sale, thinking that perhaps he can read the strange alphabet and handwritten letters that I cannot read and they will tell him what I cannot tell.

You know I don't read fairy tales anymore, he says, and gives it back to me, not even noting the year. I point to the signature on the frontispiece and he studies it. *Dan — no, Dombrowski,* he sounds out slowly. *Ger — Gergyji, Gergyji Dombrowski,* he reads the signature, *1939. Polish name, like ours — and the same year I was born,* he says. Now I too can read it plainly, and wonder that I couldn't before. But he only hands the book back to me and shrugs — *Don't know why you spend good money on this junk.*

Thereupon Hans began to whistle again and brought Wildrose shells from the beach, saying, "Hold them to your ears, little Wildrose, and these shells will tell you of my adventures when I'm gone."

But Wildrose only answered, "No, my brother, these shells speak the same false words to everyone, and so I shall not listen to their lies." Hans was not discouraged, and laughing, kissed her lips to silence them. When she was alone she took out her pine cone and grazed the rough bark of it against her cheek to try and banish her unhappiness.

Yet late that same night I swear I hear him calling me, my name, and I open the door softly, expecting him to have relented his coldness to me about the book I tried to give him. But no, he is gone. The sheets are still warm and there is a long strand of golden hair upon his pillow — her hair. I pick it up and wrap it around my finger, binding it tight.

On the day he was to go, Wildrose gave Hans the rose her mother had given her saying, "Dearest Brother, remember the promise you made Father and carry this with you always. This way you shall never lose your Wildrose, no matter where you may go in search of your fortune."

"To be sure, my little Wildrose," Hans said embracing her. "You shall never be far from my thoughts." But Wildrose was sad in her heart, for like anyone who has known the secrets of the forest, she felt the danger which lay before him, yet could not tell what it was.

In the morning he pounds on the front door to be let in. He stumbles drunkenly and there is a strangeness, a fever in his eyes. Has he eaten some of the caterer's food, I wonder? *Leave me alone,* he growls and pushes me away.

On my hands each line seems etched and inked in purple, and if one is short the other is long, but having no book to tell them by, I cannot distinguish between the lines of life, heart or head, which I know lie there because my brother had traced them by these names, many years before, on my palms. Now it's impossible to know even which side they begin, which they end, or if the small crosses interrupting them have been or will be. Even so, one line comforts me, for it so long as to traverse the length of my right palm around to the back, so that I must turn my hand over to see where it leaves off.

Outside my window, I can't help noticing how the drug-dealer is beautiful, how his legs are strong and brown, how he tosses back his hair.

Hans joined up with a wealthy ship and his willing ways and hard work earned him favor in the captain's eyes. The captain was a jovial fellow who had a great fondness for tales and drink. Every evening he invited a different member of his crew to his cabin, with the requirement that afterwards each entertain the captain with a story that had never been heard before. One evening it had come to Hans' turn, and when the captain had finished off two bottles of whiskey, he sat back in expectation of a good story, because Hans was the cleverest and most able of his men. But Hans could think of no new tale to tell; he thought and thought, and the evening grew longer for it. Finally the cap-

tain, his patience sorely taxed, banged his pipe upon the table, "Here, here," he said, "there must be something you can tell me." So Hans thought a moment longer and than began: "I am a sad and weary man."

What would you like for dinner?

As the count of earthquake victims nears 10,000, new hidden health hazards emerge for the survivors, and rescue efforts become more difficult. But as I am late in preparing dinner, I do not hear any more news. He eats, retires early, evening begins and at long last the sun sets and I begin to listen for the rustle at the door.

I always hear his breathing first, a hoarse, hollow sound, but close to words and then he turns and is silent. I open his door, slowly, holding my breath, and look at him in the light thrown in. After a time he opens his eyes and says, *What is it?* I shut the door and say in the lowest whisper that I have heard him cry out in his sleep and I wonder if he is all right. *That's funny*, he says, *for I was having a pleasant dream.*

". . . and I have journeyed far in search of a woman. She appeared in the forest one day, where I grew up; a beautiful maiden with golden hair which caught the sun and held it, even in the thickest and darkest part of the woods." And Hans told the captain of the secrets the beautiful maiden had shared with him and the fairness of her skin; how the water that touched her lips became sweet as honey and how her eyes laughed like the sea under the sun; how the animals ate from her hands and how the birds sang when she came near. "But alas, one day she disappeared, leaving only a little rose blossom which she wore in her hair upon the great rock by the river which warbled like a meadowlark." Here Hans brought the rose out of his pocket to show to the captain, who already had tears in his eyes.

What was it? I am so surprised he is actually there that I hug my long nightgown close because it will be a sign of humility that I dare ask him to tell me, knowing as I do anyway, as I have always known what he dreams. *Wouldn't you like to know.*

I go nearer to him and sit down on the bed. *I won't say anything*, I say, *you can trust me.*

I know, he sighs, *I know.* Next to him she moves a little and I see the outline of her cheek and that the sheets have fallen off during the course of the night's heat and now cling just to the toes of her left foot which crosses over his ankle and keeps it from moving. The window curtains blow out, then are sucked back against the screen. Suddenly I hear the tick, tick, tick of the drug-dealer's bicycle. He must be returning from some night meeting, some business circumstance. *What is her name?* I ask.

You better go back to bed, he says, taking my hand and biting my little finger softly, *be a good girl.*

When I open the door I look back and see specks of powder gleaming on her cheek in the light.

"So I left my home and my parents to find her again, she who has no name, only eyes that tell the sea and hair that promises the sun. But I have had no luck. I fear that fate has hardened her heart against me and that what I seek lies forever behind me."

The captain was charmed by Hans' tale and shedding a profuse number of tears he drank another half-bottle of whisky in silence. "Yet there is more to this story," the captain pronounced solemnly.

Would you like some more coffee? He puts down the newspaper and gets up to leave. This reminds me of the horoscope in my pocket and I feel for it, but it isn't there. It's gone. I try to picture the words again, but they all fall together in long, dark lines.

Then he continued, "For I believe I know the maiden of whom you speak. She of the golden hair which promises the sun, of the blue eyes which keep the sea and which in turn the sea keeps, of the sweet fair skin is my only daughter, who awaits me in the city we even now make speed towards and, willing good winds and weather, shall reach in seven day's time." The captain sucked at his pipe slowly and after a moment, he added in a somber voice, "If you find my daughter to be she whom you seek, I should be pleased to make her your wife and to welcome you as my own dearest son."

"You honor me," Hans replied, bowing his head. "With much happiness and gratitude I accept your offer."

But tonight, when I open his bedroom door he is gone again. Again, the sheets are warm, and hearing steps, I run out into the hall to catch them. Instead, who should I meet but the drug dealer, coming down, no doubt, to conduct some late night racket. From next door, at the caterer's, I hear the soft click-click of the doorknob's release. Had he been about to meet with the drug dealer?

Unbeknown to Hans, however, another sailor on the ship had spied him taking the rose out of his pocket to show to the captain, and so powerful was its perfume even he could smell it through the porthole window, and verily it brought even his own true love before his eyes. Stealthily he followed Hans when he left the captain's cabin, and when he heard Hans' snores, he crept into his quarters and stole the rose from the pocket of his coat.

Look, isn't that yours? the drug dealer points to my little green book on the floor, in front of the caterer's door.

Yes, but what is it doing there? I was certain I had not taken the book outside the apartment; it could only have been done by my brother, though I could not imagine why. He picks it up and fans through the pages.

Have you seen my brother? I ask.

He shrugs. *No. And I didn't know he was your brother — I thought he was your husband, or maybe your father.* He remains looking at me, and I understand he wants to come into the apartment and that if I didn't let him he'd whistle out of pure nervousness. *Come in,* I open the door wide. *So, what's it about, your book?* he said. *Can you read this language?*

I'll read it to you, if you like. He smiles and nods, handing it to me. *Would you like some coffee?* After all, he won't be able to tell that I'm making it up.

In seven days' time, as sure as the winds blew strong and as the sun shone fair, the captain's ship sailed into the Port of his homeland and Hans met the captain's daughter and loved her, for indeed, she was true to the captain's description and a fairer maiden could not be found. And she loved him. As for the second sailor, who had stolen the rose — he journeyed on farther into the country to reach his father's house, where he hoped to find his own true love still waiting. And wonder! For he was the very same son of the sailor that had been caring for Wildrose, and the very same young man who had first led her to his father's house. After he embraced his father, he presented her with the rose and she was filled with sadness, for she recognized it instantly. Yet Wildrose smiled at him sweetly and kissed his cheek in thanks. That night, she bundled up the few belongings she had and set off for the city.

The next day, I invited him in again, and he smoked

125

cigarettes while we drank coffee, and the smoke curled up and spread across the sunshine like a blue veil. *Let me show you,* I said, *how you might braid your hair.* His hair was truly beautiful, and I braided it with the same ornate knot the sailor upstairs had taught me. When I was done I took him to my mirror to show him. *Come to the mountains with me,* he said to me in the mirror. *There is a spot I know, by a lake as round and silver as a full moon, and we can build a fire and stay the night there and wake to the calls of the loons.* The picture he described made me tremble. *My brother would never let me,* I said. *You must follow your heart,* he answered.

The wedding took place in seven days time, and festivity and feasting the like of which have never been seen before nor since were held in honor of Hans and his bride. There were racks of lamb basted in garlic oil, strips of beef marinated in wine, hams glazed with cherries and succulent goose roasted to an even brown; there were baked flounder fillets, scalloped cod, oysters, clams, lobster tails and squid fresh from the sea and served with sweet butter and slices of lemon. There were salty black olives and almond-stuffed green ones, cheeses oozing cream and cheeses rich with blue veins. There were seven kinds of sausage. There were melons dripping honey, oranges with wine-red flesh, pomegranates splitting with seeds, copper-color pears with an aftertaste of cinnamon and figs full of golden syrup. There were white breads warm from the oven, cakes made from sesame and ground poppyseed flour, dark chocolates, and a choice of lime-green sherbet or crème-brulée. The best dark-roasted coffee, the most delicate of exotic teas, and several hundred wines of the first distinction were served.

And at the end of the evening, when the guests were merry with drink, their stomachs full with food, the captain pro-

claimed a toast to Lady Fortune, who had so graced him by bringing Hans to his ship and then to his daughter. The guests gladly raised their cups. Then the captain turned to Hans with a jovial twinkle in his eye and whispered, "My boy, now is the time to give my daughter the flower you once showed me, if only to prove she is indeed the maiden whom you have sought so long."

Later, we could ride the horses my mother keeps up there, the pinto and the little white Arab, and I could show you all the mountain trails, and I can take you to my plants, as big as me, rows and rows, thick with the sweetest bud you can imagine. And we'll breathe in the smell of the pines, and we'll think about the world, how everything is possible. But just as he finished saying this we heard a loud crash outside, and looking out we saw the caterer had dropped a set of plates which had smashed to pieces on the asphalt. *Poor guy, I'll go give him a hand,* the drug dealer said. *You think about it,* he pointed a finger at me before leaving.

But alas the rose was nowhere to be found! Hans searched here and there and then collapsed in his room weeping for shame. The captain's daughter came up to see what was wrong. "I have lost the rose," he explained to her; "you shall never have me, now." "That is no matter, for I shall go and get you another!" she answered gaily and skipped down to the garden to pluck him another rose.

In the garden below, a young maid with bright blue eyes stood watching the captain's daughter search for a rose; "Here," she said finally, "I have one and I will give it to you." "Why yes," the captain's daughter cried, "that is the perfect one! Thank you so much. Now you must come join us in our wedding feast," she said. "No, no," the girl shook her head shyly.

"But I will give you a present for your wedding. It isn't much, but here by the sea it is a rare thing," and she drew out a pine cone from the folds of her dress.

Hans was delighted. It seemed as if the captain's daughter had found the very same rose he had lost! But in her excitement the captain's daughter forgot to show Hans the pine cone, and it rolled under the bed unnoticed.

For the first time I go into his room while the sun is still bright. I open the curtains. The sheets are rumpled and I push my face into them, trying to smell him; but there is only the scent I know already — sweet, strong; the perfume which I have so often smelled in the windowless air of the hall.

When the happy couple returned to the feast some would swear the rose bloomed anew in the new brides' hair, and its sweet breath grew so strong that all the guests, even in the farthest reaches of the room, inhaled its incense and raised their cups to the gracious omen.

The sailor is coming to my door again, I can hear the limp on the stair, now the wheels of the vacuum.

Have you reconsidered? he asks. The woman tattooed on his arm flashes brightly, the colors sharp, and he grins to see me look at her. *Have you changed your mind about a demonstration?*

At long last, Hans and his bride retired to his bedchamber, blissful in their love. But during the night, as his bride slept soft and still on his breast, the moon rose high and its light fell upon Hans' face and awoke him. He looked at his little bride, sleeping so quiet in its light, and lo! it was Little Wildrose herself, and Hans felt her arms tighten about him in response to his waking, her lips press close to his skin, and Hans touched her cheek and fell asleep once again.

You will not regret this, he smiles as he comes in. *Take me to a bedroom, if you don't mind, for it is there the Yorick proves itself most admirably.* I decide to take him to my brother's bedroom; why not? The sailor strips the sheets off his bed and applies the vacuum to his mattress. Like magic, layers of muck are whisked up into a clear plastic container where they can be seen plainly. *You see?* he says, and I must concede.

In the morning, when the servants knocked at their door to wake them for breakfast, there was no answer, and the servants smiled and gossiped among themselves. But when the sun began to sink once more into the sea, the servants became worried and said to one another, "It is all very well, but we must know when to serve them their supper; there are too many things to be done than to pass the day waiting on the leisure of young lovers." Imagine their surprise and horror when, opening the door, they found Hans and his bride thickly entwined in the thorny vines of a wildrose, and the room overwhelmed with the sweet smell of a hundred pink blossoms, so profuse that they covered the young lovers' flesh from the servants' eyes. But no petal stirred, for they did not breathe to stir them; and if the young man and his fair bride slept smiling, so it was the sleep of death.

May I use it now? My brother can give you a check when he comes home tonight. The sailor smiles. *Of course. Enjoy yourself,* he winks. *Thank you,* I hold out my hand, remembering my manners. Once he is gone, I begin vacuuming.

But even as the servants gazed upon them in their innocent tranquility, the clay tiles upon which they stood began to heave and it seemed the whole city trembled, the bells clanging out in thunderous peals, and shouts of fear ascended from the

streets.

"God in heaven help us," the servants prayed, yet the shaking grew stronger and a moment later the earth yawned open beneath them and swallowed their appeals, the pretty whitewashed villa and all its swaying palm trees between its teeth. And then the sea rose up in a mighty swell, spread itself across the farthest reaches of the city and drew back again, leaving no one left to tell.

I vacuumed every nook and cranny in that apartment; I vacuumed high and low; I tried out each and every one of the ten different attachments. When the first bag was full, I changed it, and then I filled another.

By the time he came I had everything vacuumed clean as a whistle, so I could leave knowing I'd done my best by him — if nothing else.